CROSSINGS 20

A Season in Florida

A Season in Florida

Stories

Emanuele Pettener

Translated from the Italian by

Thomas De Angelis

BORDIGHERA PRESS

Library of Congress Control Number: 2014944622

Cover Photo: Ilaria Chiaruzzi
Art Design: Francesca Serra

Published by
BORDIGHERA PRESS
John D. Calandra Italian American Institute
25 West 43rd Street, 17th Floor
New York, NY 10036

CROSSINGS 20
ISBN 978-1-59954-054-2

TABLE OF CONTENTS

ACKNOWLEDGMENTS

"The Incredible Story of John Cavallaro" is unpublished; "The Night I Became a Real Man" and "The Complete Works of Ellery Queen" were published in Italian in *Nuova Prosa* and in English in *Big Pulp;* "A Season in Florida" was also published in *Nuova Prosa*, in Italian, and, in English, in *Sliptongue*; "A Pointed Finger" is unpublished in English, while in Italian inspired and became part the novel *Proust per bagnanti* (Meligrana, 2013); "Portrait in Green with Proust" has been published in Italian in *Prospektiva* and in English in *The Mississippi Crow*; "Revelations," published by *Ellin Selae* in Italian, is unpublished in English. The stories published in the United States were translated by Tom di Salvo; all the translations here, by Thomas De Angelis, are, instead, completely new.

While not fond of public acknowledgments in any part of a book, I do feel the urgency to express my deep gratitude to two friends: Thomas De Angelis for his wonderful work; and Anthony Julian Tamburri, who made my American Dream possible, and keeps making it. *Grazie!*

A Season in Florida

Stories

The Night I Became A Real Man

The night I became a real man, well, I still remember it.

Mestre, my city, the most beautiful city in the world, was brisk that spring night, its trees still bare, it was only ten o'clock at night, maybe a little later, but there was no one on the streets, just the light glowing from streetlamps and closed shutters, the ground bathed in a sheen after a cool and intoxicating misty rain, the air heady with the perfume of mimosas.

Marta, a young woman I had met at the university, came to pick me up, she was having boyfriend troubles, or something like that. She had on a tiny black miniskirt and black stockings, which looked nice on her, even though she was short and not even that pretty. She wore very thick glasses, had a large pronounced nose and a pleasant, smiling, ordinary looking little face.

"You coming down?" She asked loudly, and I, leaning out of the window of my parents' apartment, said: "yes."

Marta had a red Citroën 2CV and she drove deftly, gripping the shift with a kind of erotic determination, while her black-stockinged legs danced between the clutch and the brakes, this small young woman seemed like an amazon who had tamed her stallion and I envied her, yes I envied her, and so I wanted her.

"Where are we going?" She asked me, it was unsettling that she managed to talk, wear black nylons *and* change gears – God, what a one-woman wonder!

"What do you think about going to Tropical?"

Tropical was about a hundred yards from the hospital, behind the railroad tracks, and it was a bar convinced it was a Miami Beach nightclub: the trains whistled in the distance, the walls were painted in Caribbean colors, with palm trees and sand and ocean, the manager had a nice smile and always wore a Hawaiian shirt, the customers (for the most part lanky young men and colorful girls) seemed like surfing veterans who needed margaritas and chili, as the sound of Key West's Jimmy Buffet singing *Cheeseburger in Paradise* reverberated from the speakers.

Marta parked, maneuvering the car with minimal ease into a space between a black Mercedes and a purple BMW, and as she turned the key to switch the engine off she said, "here we are," and spread her legs to open the door – and I felt a pang of remorse in the pit of my stomach.

But Marta seemed a little too happy for having just ended a five year relationship, at twenty years old that's an eternity, I realized it when she ordered a double shot of whiskey, "hey, you're a tough little cookie, huh?"

"Tonight I want to pull out all the stops," she whispered, cracking a mischievous smile.

"Sounds good to me, but don't forget you have to drive home."

Marta lived in the countryside, in a kind of old granary that had been transformed into a small castle, I had already been there for a party, overflowing with tequila, a lot of dogs and very comfortable couches.

"Worst case scenario *you* take me home and *you* keep the car," she said sticking her nose into the whisky glass.

I froze.

The strange side effect of the whisky was that her glasses fogged up, so she took them off, revealing two large eyes, circles under them the color of tortoise shells and tree bark, staring right back at me, maybe she was expecting a compliment.

"You have beautiful eyes. I'm impressed."

"Look, when I drink I can't handle compliments."

"Why what happens?"

"Hmm."

What a conversation. God, who's scripting this for us, a soap opera digest writer? Anyway my concentration was riveted on her stockings, they seemed delicate and soft, and the girl had her legs crossed voluptuously under the table. I took my sweet time sipping my Corona, just like the tough guys do, then all of a sudden I noticed she had a vacant look in her eyes, I wasn't sure at first if this was some ploy to reassert her dignity or if the whisky had already turned her brain to mush or if the ghost of her ex had suddenly resurfaced.

"What's wrong Marta, you meditating?"

"Thinking, more than anything else…."

"That's the positive side of whisky. It makes you think."

"No, it's just… I was thinking."

"Okay."

"I was with Urbano for five years, and now I'm here flirting with you."

"Urbano? What a name! Usually men named Urbano are insufferable."

"Come on!" And she pretended to slap me.

"Sorry. Do you want to talk about it?"

"No."

"Okay."

"Such is life."

"That's what my grandmother always says. And she also says, "life's a bitch.""

"Your grandmother is wise."

"My grandmother!? Hearing my mother's take on it, she's been a birdbrain since she was twenty."

Here I assumed she'd laugh, instead she started crying. The night was careening down a slippery slope. I have never been any great comfort to the brokenhearted (not even if they're wearing black nylons). I didn't understand either why she was so upset over someone named Urbano, I watched her tears streaming down the sides of her big nose and all I could manage to do was massage her shoulders and say, "come on, don't do this to yourself," along with a few other trite sayings. So she told me her story, it seems that Urbano was a suntanned gym rat whose specialty was IT, Information Technology. He was a great lover and a collector of vintage models, they had known each other since they were kids and always got along really well but then something set her off, *he no longer knew how to thrill her* – "excuse me, but in the beginning how did he thrill you?" – *Well I don't know, you know, with little things*, and they had started to fight over the most stupid things, they didn't even need a reason to argue, and she couldn't stand it that he was so *inflexible and immature and self satisfied.* He didn't understand that she had other needs, *that she needed to grow* and instead, with him *she felt inhibited, stymied, she felt like she was suffocating* – "and what did your growth consist of and what were the insidious ways that the brute wanted to clip your wings?" – *YesYesYes, clip my wings, you've understood me perfectly, that's what he was doing, even if unconsciously so, yeah, I can't deny it.*

If I play my cards right I can pull this off, I thought, with my old beautiful hard standard at attention and the background music oozing sadness.

We left. The night was cool and comfortable. The train was whistling and there was perfume floating in the air. To get to where the car was parked, we had to cross a tiny wooden footbridge over a small stream – it was there that I grabbed her, her shoulders were like a baby bird's, vigorously I reeled her around, and kissed her.

She succumbed to me like dead weight, it was a very perfunctory kiss, I realized, something that had to be done but maybe in another place at another time – but I was young, by God, and the night was beautiful, and I wanted this girl!

We moved away from each other and our whisky and beer breaths blended into a singular face-to-face banter, "I didn't think that you would make a move this quickly…," she whispered in a throaty voice.

"Kissing you?" I asked in the same throaty voice.

"Hmm."

"You seemed so vulnerable to me...."

"What does that mean, you kissed me because you felt sorry for me?"

"Well no, not because you were in pain, out of tenderness if anything."

I kissed her on her white neck and ran my hand over her back (but the fabric was coarse and the motion wasn't fluid) and she closed her eyes sighing and ran her fingers through my hair – but neither of us seemed completely convinced.

"Shall we go somewhere and talk?" I asked her, a bit distractedly.

"Another bar?"

"Even in the car...."

She flashed a beautiful smile and gave me a smack on the lips, "it's a little too soon for *talking* in the car, don't you think?"

Damn, she caught me with my pants down. I felt my cheeks flush bright red, I tried to stay cool and kissed her again and pulled her against me so she'd feel the virility of my lust – but she gently put her hand on my chest and said, "we've already taken this a little past what I usually consider acceptable for a first date...."

I blushed again, "sorry, I didn't mean to offend you."

"Oh, I'm not offended, by any means...."

"It's just, I like you."

"And I like you."

So screw it, let's hook up! Life is short! It's spring! I'm so turned on! I want to rip off your stockings with my teeth and gulp you down whole like a morsel of fried chicken!

"I think it's better if we just go home," she concluded with a smile that said it all.

"Yeah, maybe it's better that way," I sighed, trotting out my worst passport photo smile of all time.

She turned the car on, shifted into reverse, looked at me, I placed my hand on her tiny black-sheathed knee, she left it there, but she had to shift gears and I thought it would be better if I removed my hand.

I was pissed off and horny, and I needed to say something but I could only think of how she would look naked, of how small and firm her breasts must be, like two little rocks, and how fantastically furry her crotch must be, her hard, pink rear – and I thought that, in the end, it was a waiting game, it was only our first time out, it was a question of being discreet, "When can we see each other again?"

Silence. I had a handle on my nerves. I tried to better explain myself, "because I had a nice time with you and I'd like to see you again."

"I don't know."

"Tomorrow?"

"Tomorrow … no … tomorrow I can't."

"I understand."

"It's just that… you see… tonight I realized how much I'm still hung up on Urbano… and it doesn't seem right for me to be here with you, so soon…"

"It's called a guilt trip. But you shouldn't be fooled into feeling guilty, it's tricky, the last-ditch attempt by the con artist that we call our conscience."

"Why is our conscience a con artist?"

"Because it passes off cowardly actions as moral ones."

"So then I'm a coward?"

"We all are, my friend. We're afraid to cut our ties with the past, because basically the past is all we have. Whatever connection you have with Urbano, or whatever the hell his name is, is a magnificent past, but truth be told it's magnificent because it's over and you've forgotten about it, probably at the time it didn't seem so wonderful to you."

"But we shared so many dreams together!"

"Namely, the future. Look, what ties you to him is a past that doesn't exist and a future that will never happen. And in the name of something inexistent, our conscience urges you not to live a concrete present and, let me say that, an appealing one."

"Maybe because it's not right."

"Or maybe because you're afraid that I, Urbano, you yourself and the world in general will judge you as an ungrateful, superficial, air head: five years with Urbano and poof, suddenly you're kissing the first guy who shows up on a picture perfect spring night. But I have to wonder: why do we attach such a fatal and ridiculous moral importance to the past? Why are five years more important than one night? I'm convinced that that damn Viennese doctor had something to do with it!"

But the wet road was slippery and Marta went around the S curve going from Piazza Barche to Via Forte Marghera too fast and the red *deux chevaux* went straight ahead (luckily there was no one else in the oncoming lane), Marta slammed on the breaks and the car spun around a couple of times before landing on the sidewalk with a heavy thud. Thank God, there wasn't another soul around.

I looked at Marta and Marta looked at me – and in her wild eyes I sensed a terrified look – and only in that moment did I feel my heart racing in my chest, and the more I saw her mouth, tense and turned downward, the more I felt a knot deep in my stomach, and the images of the city whirling around me were flashing dizzily through my head. Then she passed out and I calmed down. I somehow realized that we were safe and I had to act like a man: besides her skirt had been hiked up so high that I could see her black underwear beneath her tights. I thought I could make a virtue out of necessity. I thought she would be grateful if I could alleviate some of her fear. I slapped her with a renewed optimism, while outside it began to drizzle, the streetlights lit up the empty roads, a cat meowed and two cars passed by, indifferent, probably thinking that being parked on the sidewalk was unwise but temporary, that maybe we had stopped for a quickie or were saying a long goodnight to each other.

Then Marta came to. She looked at me as if she had just come out of her mother's womb. She was dazed. I gently caressed her and told her that everything would be all right, that nothing had happened, that she would be fine and some other reassuring clichés – in the meantime I was looking at the hem of her black stockings which had formed a magical circle around the delicate thighs of this filly, and the small black triangle in the middle of her open legs was candidly exposed. I wanted to dive into it head first! But maybe she would have found that too insensitive.

"I'm such an idiot!" And those were the first words she said.

"It could have happened to anyone, the streets are wet and slippery."

"And it's raining again!"

I thought she was going to start crying, so I said, "shall we go to a bar and get something strong to drink?"

She seemed a bit pissed, "maybe I've already had to much to drink, ya think?"

She closed her legs, pulled her skirt down. We got out to check the car. There was no damage. We were about to get into the car, when she said, "can *you* drive, please?"

And that's when I freaked out, my heart galloping like a bay horse at sundown, I stood perfectly still in the rain (which didn't even faze me).

This is the story. I didn't drive. Driving had always terrified me: better to jump into a crate full of poisonous snakes, than drive. Better to face King Kong on a day when he was in a bad mood, than drive. Better to be naked in Siberia in the dead of winter or to wear a heavy sweater in the tropics during the summer, than drive. I think I've made my point. Oh yeah, I did get a driver's license!

And it was the most wonderful day of my life. Never had a college exam or seducing a girl or whatever success I had attained up until that moment – I was a smart guy, with no other complexes – given me as much profound happiness. It took me three years. For three years I made my parents spend thousands of liras on driving school lessons, I failed driving tests and terrorized driving instructors, I gave up countless times and shamefully wept in the corner of my bedroom – until finally my exasperated father forcibly put me behind the wheel of his grey Honda Civic. Every time was torture: every part of my body was paralyzed and sweat dripped icily down the inside of my shirt while my father sat next to me saying, "turn on the engine… foot on the clutch… no, that's the break!… Good… put it in reverse… take your foot off the clutch and slowly put your foot on the gas…"

Christ, how was it possible for me to remember all that minutiae!!! My brain transmitted it all to my feet with disarming sluggishness and frequently in a language my feet didn't understand and I was like a stuffed bird in traffic – the traffic! What tremendous anguish!!! To me the other cars seemed like enormous monsters that just barely missed grazing the gigantic piece of metal whose cockpit I was in, and from one moment to the next it seemed to me that they were going to crash into me killing me once and for all.

One day at the YIELD sign at the end of viale San Marco, where San Giuliano begins, I saw a Fiat 500, menacing and ominous, approaching suddenly on the left. It was actually pretty far away, I would have had time to get out of the car, go to a café, have a sandwich, drink a cup of coffee and in the end come back and see the ugly monster dart in front of me – but I slammed on the brakes to be on the safe side and BAM! The blue VW Golf behind us unceremoniously rear-ended me.

(Oh, Persephone and Hades, why didn't you intervene then and take me out of this world like you would pluck a useless ugly flower, why didn't you open up the abyss that could have gently swallowed me whole?)

I didn't dare look at my father, I think I saw him turn bright red from anger and shame because of his idiot son – but my father always had this distinctive idiosyncrasy of getting angry at the stupidest things and being as cool as a cucumber in stressful situations. He took my wrist, no pulse, and murmured in the calmest voice in the world, "Relax, nothing bad happened."

I remained behind the wheel, wishing I could vanish into thin air, my heart pulverized, my head exploding, and in the rear view mirror I witnessed the following scene: the driver of the blue VW Golf, a woman about fifty-five years old, dumbfounded, got out of her car, was appalled looking at her bumper (there was a broken headlight, but no major damage) then she looked at the rear bumper of the Civic (dented) and finally at my father (whose kind face fully expressed his regret, he stood there with his arms wide-open: "what can you do?"). The woman stammered, "but...but...why did he stop?"

"Madame, there was a car that was suddenly approaching us on the right."

"But... but... it was so far away!"

"Madame, you can never be too careful."

"But there's careful and *careful*, look at this..."

"Madame, you see the **P**? My son is practicing his driving..."

"Yes, but for a beginner he's not too bright at all! The Fiat was in Canada!"

Here's the thing with my Dad, unflappable up until then: as soon as someone picks on his son and doubts his intellectual capacity (a more than legitimate doubt) his voice becomes strained and his jaw tenses up, "look, you worry about keeping an appropriate distance behind a vehicle and *I'll* deal with my son. So, can we exchange our insurance papers with some civility?"

And they did. My father got back into the car quite content, howling derisively, "hee! Hee! Hee! We just got the bumper fixed!"

"But we didn't need to!"

"Well, there were a few scratches".

"But the car really was in Canada...."

"No, in Canada no, let's say New York! Hee! Hee! Hee! Come on, turn the car on so we can go!"

"We're leaving? Dad, I can't do it, I'm in shock!"

"Just go, you pussy!"

And we left, and not long after that, a month before my date with Marta, my stomach all in knots and the veins in my neck bulging, on the verge of a mental meltdown, I got through the written test and the practical as well. I remember that we went down a street full of potholes and I didn't miss hitting even one and the test monitor, an easy-going old guy sitting in the back seat, said to me, "have a thing for potholes, do we?" My father was sitting next to me and laughed his ass off and the monitor also laughed heartily and I tried to laugh but something like *ha ha* came out, so I said, "sorry, I realize I'm a bit nervous, normally I'm never so uptight." The monitor fell for it and told me, "it's okay, come back to the office and sign the paperwork and you'll have your license in about a month." As for me, as soon as the guy left, I cried, hugging my Dad.

But a month went by and I hadn't driven at all and in my heart I had decided never to drive again. What did it matter? The license, a baby-pink color that made me passionately delirious every time I slipped it out of my wallet as I admired the back and the front of it, the license conferred social respectability on me, officially confirming that I wasn't a loser (I was like everyone else, I was a driver!) – *I had* a license. Here it is, guys, shining like a peach blossom on a beautiful spring sky: so if I don't drive it's because I don't like to, it's boring, and traffic is unnerving – but *I could.* I'm a non-conformist, I don't need to drive to prove my masculinity, quite the opposite, I love women who drive – I was born to compose short madrigals sitting next to a cute little blond who's tearing up the road at 70 miles an hour.

And now, in the cold and relentless rain, Marta was looking at me, sensing my uneasiness, maybe she thought that I didn't feel like driving all the way out to the country. I took my time and asked her, "but how will *I* get home?"

Her face was wet from the rain and her tears, but she didn't seem to notice, grabbing her whole body as if she were cold or at the end of her rope, "yeah, you're probably right…"

"I'm really sorry, I would gladly drive you, no problem…" I said, greatly relieved.

"I'll call my father to come pick me up…"

I was embarrassed. I felt that I was bailing, leaving her helpless, that I had to do something. Plus her mother and father were really rather old.

"Wait a sec. You're going to call home in the middle of the night and make your father come all the way out here? Look, in a few minutes you'll be less anxious, you'll see, I feel better already, and besides if you don't get back in the car now you run the risk of not wanting to ever drive again, you have to face the effects of the shock head on…"

I went over to her and went through the motions like I was going to hug her, and then she dove into my arms and started sobbing, "I was *so* afraid…"

"I know, I know…"

Then she looked up at me, like a little kitten, and said, "how about if *you* drive, tonight you can sleep at my house and tomorrow I'll bring you home?"

Once again I had that sinking sensation of two huge claws clutching my heart, ending up in the pit of my stomach, I had been blindsided and I knew it. I looked at her and I wanted to tell her that, dammit, I would love to but I had a very early appointment the next morning – but I couldn't be such a wuss. I looked around, the rain was pelting the glistening puddles, shining in the light of the streetlamps, the closed gas stations and the small boats moored at the docks in the Salso Canal (the skuzziest little river in the world, a greasy armpit full of huge grey rats, foul-smelling, being upwind from Marghera). Marta looked at me beseechingly as I held her in my arms, terrified, while strangers slept peacefully in their little brick houses, deaf to the dark roaring of my heart and the intermittent meowing of the cats, the soundtrack of this nocturnal nightmare – and then I caved in and whispered, "okay."

Like a condemned criminal approaching the gallows, that's how I got into the car with my brain sending me flashes from the hereafter, where I continued to ask Marta to forgive me since I was responsible for both of us drowning in the Salso Canal, before our carcasses were scarfed down by rats.

Right foot on the clutch, I thought, and left foot lightly touching the gas pedal.

My heart was beating to the rhythm of a thousand drums. I put the key in the ignition, turned on the car, and an electrifying shock shot through my chest. The street was still empty and slick, and it was raining. God, at least make it stop raining, I prayed.

Marta fiddled with a knob and turned the windshield wipers on. I shifted into reverse to the jarring sound of grinding gears, "happens all the time," said Marta. I eased up on the clutch with the accuracy of a surgeon and slowly put my foot on the gas, too slowly, the car stalled, "it stalls all the time", added Marta again. I was wondering if she could hear my nerves squealing, if she suspected that I was scared shitless. Fuck, I said, fuck – a word that has always given me courage. I turned the car on again, stepping on the gas, the engine roared, moved ahead, a weight lifted from my heart, every part of my body loosened up, I was reeling from the blood circulating, a drop of urine stained my boxers and I clenched my sphincter muscles. With a thud the car fell off the sidewalk, when all of a sudden two far away headlights sucked my heart, my limbs and my blood into a vortex, and I put both feet on the brake and the clutch, in a split second I remembered about the clutch, and I understood that the car would stall again so I slammed my left foot on the clutch and – miraculously! – the engine didn't conk out, instead it snarled, muttering like an indecisive bulldog debating whether he should sic 'em or should sit still.

The car took an incredible amount of time to pass us, it was a blue Skoda all banged up and peaceful, as languid as a self-satisfied seal, I stared at it with a mixture of hate and relief, then I apologized awkwardly, "it was in Canada, I know, I took a lot of time passing it, but with what's happened, I'm taking it easy…"

She laughed, and also seemed relieved, "Oh, you don't have to make any excuses, and I really thank you so much, I don't know how you can be so calm and collected, driving after what happened."

No you don't really know, my friend.

The car moved along with its requisite French finesse, the bulldog seemed to have been tamed, I managed to get back into my lane and I thought that it was time to shift into second – so I went over in my head what I had to do, not without swearing to myself for encouragement: I felt drops of sweat lapping at my temples when I put my foot on the clutch again and, confidently, but without rancor, shoved the gearshift – and did it, yes I did it, by God, I was in second and the car moved ahead and once again my chest relaxed, relieved, and I couldn't help but sigh.

"Everything all right?" I asked Marta almost fishing for a compliment.

"Super." And I believe she smiled, just the same I didn't dare take my eyes off the road.

It was already time to shift into third, the bulldog was starting to snarl, but the traffic light on Via Sansovino forced me to stop before making a left turn and then, right there, something chilling happened: in back of us there was another car. I saw the headlights, cold and cynical, doubtful and distrustful of my ability. I was sweating and was afraid of pissing my pants. Another car behind me had always been the worst possible thing, I felt like I was being judged, expecting that at any moment the horn would start honking, looking at the rear view mirror and always seeing an enraged and scornful face. But my father used to tell me: *Let us not speak of them, but look, and pass*[1] he would say, because, if he could, he always came up with something worth quoting.

And so I didn't let it get to me, or pretended not to, but fate ambushed me. I had done everything just fine, I kept the motor running at the red light, when the light turned green I proceeded, the car a little zippy, then in the opposite direction two jaguar eyes opened in the night and I understood that it was a dangerous animal, not like the old Skoda from before, but still this one was far away, I was certain it was far away, I was certain that had I stopped I would have looked like an idiot, that the car behind me would honk its horn exposing my cowardly soul or would have even crashed into me like the woman in the VW – and so I went on, by God, I stepped on the gas pedal that was screaming joyfully and I passed it. Then I turned easily and got back into the lane as if the car were a triumphant chariot and I, in the euphoria, immediately shifted into second and then third, and we were rolling along, yes we were rolling along at a good clip, and I was tempted to look at Marta, to see if she could feel my heart exploding, if she was amazed by my bravery, if she were expecting me to be that special breed of driver….

But Marta said nothing and I calmed down, I knew all too well that I was acting like an asshole and that the trip was still a long one.

At Viale San Marco, where I live, I managed to shift into fourth and my heart was singing a tenor's aria: Good God, why isn't there anyone around to see me?

But I was really concentrating.

Marta said, "I still don't understand why I took that curve so fast, I really am an idiot!"

"No you're not, come on."

---

[1] Dante, *Inferno*, canto III.

"It must have been the whisky, you shouldn't have let me drink like that."

"No, really, let it go."

"I want to ask you to excuse me, I hope that you can forgive me, and I really don't know how to thank you and…"

At any other time those words and her hand placed unexpectedly above my right knee, even though both were the result of her apprehension and gratitude and not flirting, would have aroused my most perverse thoughts – but at that very moment I was deaf, and her affectionate hand on my thigh was nothing but an annoying nuisance for my leg, tensed to the last muscle, performing its duty. Luckily she removed it immediately and I, gaining more self confidence, felt that the car was letting itself be controlled and I even went over an overpass, with me driving, by God, I continued switching gears without a hitch and I drove as if hypnotized, ecstatic, and I began to feel happy almost to the point of having my insides explode.

"But do you always drive like that, with your back arched over the wheel?" Asked Marta.

"What?" And I turned my head to look at her. I swear I did it. And I realized that I could take my eyes off the road and look at her, and it was phenomenal that it was really *me*, yes, I was driving like every other human being who knew how to drive and at the same time was carrying on a conversation with the person sitting next to him. I was so stoked by the latest discovery that I turned to her four times in the short span of time it took to utter the following sentence: "no – it's just that – with the rain – I – can't see that well." I sounded like an epileptic.

We came to Terraglio, the large broad street that leads toward the fields and then ends in Treviso, considered extremely dangerous because of the high number of all the drunken imbeciles who drive on it and crash into each other, killing dozens of defenseless people who happen to be on this road by chance, especially on weekend nights.

Just thinking about that fact, I felt a trickle of warm urine soak my boxers and a cold shiver momentarily paralyze my heart: but I would do it, by God, I would do it, not paying attention to anyone else, just as my father used to tell me.

And Terraglio, which cut through the dark countryside smelling of wet leaves, had lots of cars crisscrossing it, the headlights blinded my eyes, and I kept my distance from a black jalopy that easily blended in with the night, and in the rear view mirror I saw two headlights at a reasonable but not alarming distance, not encroaching on my space, staying comfortably behind me.

And I drove on, yes, I was driving judiciously placing my foot on the accelerator so I wouldn't be considered one of those annoying drivers on Saturday nights who holds up traffic like an old slowpoke, and as my nerves became calmer, my heart rate slowed down, my insides stopped acting up – I felt like a man for the first time.

I had never felt like a man and it was the most amazing feeling, my body language had a completely different resoluteness, my expression was virile, an adult heart was boisterously beating in my chest. But I was tooting my own horn too soon.

Suddenly, weeping willows were bending over the sides of the road, the rain had for the most part stopped, Marta had turned off the windshield wipers and everything seemed to be progressing astonishingly well, but I was forced to slow down because of a tractor stuck in front of me, its two red tail lights as small as mice minus any sense of inferiority. At first I didn't think it was that serious and I came up behind him with all the patience and indulgence in the world. That little man in the straw hat straddling that contraption reminded me of a seraphic maharajah sitting on a serene elephant's back, both of whom were right out of Rudyard Kipling's *The Jungle Book*, such faraway tales in space and time, flavored with mystery and indolence, no cars no frenzy no horns honking – then Marta blurted out,

"Check out this one, no way you can ride around on that at this hour of the night, he's gotta be drunk!"

"Who knows?"

"Oh my God, tonight it's all happening to us, you barely have room to pass him."

Once again I felt my stomach muscles contract.

"Pass him? But there's a solid line, it's a no passing zone!"

And in fact the solid line was reassuring, it seemed to settle the question once and for all and I was deeply grateful it was there.

"Fine, you've never crossed a solid line to pass anyone before?"

"Well!"

"Look, look, there's no one, pass him!"

"But... but Marta wait a sec... there's always a lot of cops around, especially on nights like this..."

Her voice was shrill and it was grating on my nerves, "yeah, but look behind us, we're the first in a line of cars, they're gonna start honking at you!"

"At me!?"

"At you, at you, they're expecting you to pass him, aren't they?"

And I looked into the rear view mirror, at the headlights of the black wreck, behind him there was another set of headlights, then another set and still more, it's true, there was a long line and they were all waiting for me to make a move, the road was narrow and dark, a tight space, you had to pass one at a time and it was up to me to go first. No one was coming in the opposite direction, dammit, and I felt my temples throbbing and my heart racing like some whack job running up and down the beach, so I started to move toward the median line, "what are you doing, not on the curve!"

"Hey, hey, calm down, I was only looking, don't get your panties in a wad, *I know* how to drive!"

She was mortified.

"Sorry...."

"Forget it."

Then the sound of a horn ripped through me like a sword thrust in my chest, it must have been the black jalopy, the traitor, and in the rear view mirror I saw the line of headlights getting longer waiting for me to move. I looked ahead, the guy with the straw hat looked like a statue and he continued to drive his tractor with glacial indifference in the dark and wet night, he looked like a demi-god in a straw hat, a demi-god sent to test my mettle, and the black and powerful trees on both sides of the road were giants who were sneering at me, and I looked at the straight stretch of road ahead of me. I eased out, went over the median line, pulled up alongside the tractor – and I did this very slowly, very slowly, by God, and in that moment in the distance two headlights suddenly appeared in front of me like two dragon's eyes and I felt a sharp kitchen knife slash my gut and it hit me that I was in fifth gear and my father had told me to always pass in second or third gear, I downshifted into third, the car let out an astounding roar, for a second I was under the impression that the maharajah stared at me agreeing with my decision as I left him in the dust, got back into the right lane, the dragon was still pretty far away, I had passed the tractor.

My back felt frozen stiff. My heart was jumping insanely like a poor freshly caught fish – then little by little my nerves calmed, the fish flopped its tail for the last time, every muscle in my body surrendered languidly, free from any anxiety, and I felt a heavenly bliss completely envelop me. I shifted into fourth, on autopilot now. Without even thinking about it. Judging from Marta's silence I understood that I had done something absolutely normal, but deep down inside me I knew that I had slain the dragon, knocked off the giants, silenced the demi-god. One after the other the cars behind me passed the tractor and were following me, but I wasn't afraid of them anymore, they couldn't judge me any more, they were fine with following me if they wanted to, they could pass me if I was going too slowly for their tastes, they might even honk at me: *Let us not speak of them, but look, and pass.*

In no time at all I turned into the dark street that led to Marta's house, the road, paved with small stones, shone yellow in the headlights and to me it seemed like a magical path that would lead me into a fairy tale, and then I veered onto an unpaved path and parked, with a spontaneity that beguiled me, in front of Marta's farmhouse. I would have liked to stay there all night, a night when I noticed marvelous colors and aromas, and I heard crickets singing chorales to me and the swishing of the wet greenery was gently rocking me like a lullaby. I looked at the amber colored sky and I imagined the mysterious life in the woods, I fantasized that the owls, the wolves, the elves and the fairies were spontaneously throwing a party in my honor.

I got out of the car and the smell of straw and manure was ambrosia, I put my arm around Marta's waist and we went into the little castle like a king with his queen.

Marta's mother and father, an elderly couple, were certainly a wizard and a good witch, he was tall and very thin and his nose looked like a small strawberry, she was small and plump and her smile was shaped like a slice of melon, they had woken up and welcomed us, a little dazed and worried, but they were brimming with kindness and concern, almost as if they had already known – it must have been the crystal ball. All four of us got comfortable on a wonderful crescent shaped green, pink and burgundy sofa in front of the fireplace.

They made the most frightening faces when we told them what had happened, then they were so very relieved and thanked God (in my opinion, they were thanking Beelzebub) and the lady witch made us chamomile tea and the old wizard lit his pipe, complimenting me a thousand times over for maintaining my composure and for my being so thoughtful.

I loved that old couple. I loved the world, I loved life, I loved that fairytale house with the cloth sunflowers hanging on the yellow walls, the light blue distillers on the mantelpiece above the fireplace, the white gauze curtains and the spiral staircase that led to the rooms upstairs, I loved the pounding night rain, the fresh aromas which wafted in from outside – I even loved Marta.

By that time it was four o'clock in the morning and suddenly I remembered that my parents would worry if they didn't hear me come home, so I asked if I could make a call. I dragged them out of bed, they were terribly frightened, and my mother screamed, "thank God, I was afraid that something happened to you involving the car."

Oh, that's exactly what happened!

Marta showed me to the guest room, we climbed the spiral staircase and went into a little room painted crimson, it had a small bed overflowing with stuffed animals: bears, crocodiles, even a spotted grey baby pig. I never really like stuffed animals, but there I felt a sense of universal tenderness.

Marta said "thanks" again and hugged me demurely.

I reciprocated by hugging her back letting out a loud belly laugh, "for what, for what!"

And this was how we said good night to each other.

I leaned out of the window of the room, it was a type of hole made in the inner tower of a castle. Below I could just make out, between the layers of fog, the living room dimly lit by candles which were still burning. There was a large table in dark wood with chairs covered in purple fabric, a place where the good wizard and his wife the witch used to drink wine in springtime when the sun was mild, and where they would dine with their gnome friends on warm summer evenings. Up ahead, I guessed was the hen house, and in front of that what must have been the original barn, where as a young man the wizard used to feed the cows and deliver their calves, before he definitively devoted himself to alchemy. A large peach tree protected the old barn, surrounded by thorny rose bushes and shrubs and fruit trees and flowers and cages for raising rabbits and beehives and troughs for the pigs – and I could barely see it all, prompted by my sheer bliss and how peaceful I felt, but the light of dawn transformed the sky into a white, pink and grey mattress and it now helped me to see even further: there, there beyond the small gate was my car, the car that had deflowered me, that had made me a man among men! How beautiful it was, how well I had parked it!

And there was this venerable countryside redolent of the dawn which was already spread out before me: the thick forest rustling with secrets and streams of water, and then the fields, the sweeping sprawl of the vineyards, the rows of tomatoes, strips of plowed red dirt. And further still was the road, the road to which I now belonged, that was no longer my enemy, the road with cars that crisscrossed each other, and among these would also be mine.

The night which had consecrated me as a man was almost over, ending hastily like all beautiful things do. It was six o'clock, a rooster crowed, and I smiled because tomorrow I would take my father's Honda Civic, tell him we were going for a ride and he would say "what a marvel"![2] I was smiling ear to ear as I slipped between the linen sheets, under the red and yellow comforter, I hugged the spotted baby pig, and I fell asleep.

---

[2] Dante, *Inferno*, canto XV.

The Incredible Story of Joe Cavallaro

The impact of the incredible story of Joe Cavallaro (who in his day stirred up quite a shit storm) has by now subsided with the years and the dust it's collected, so much so that the only reminder of Joe is a simple stone plaque, red-hot in the Miami sun, that no one places flowers in front of, no one sheds a tear for him. Personally, I knew nothing about the guy. One rainy night an old Jewish lawyer told me Joe's story while I was hanging out at a bar; he related it very slowly, the more glasses of scotch I poured him the less I believed him – but in the following months, seized by the demons of curiosity, I collected some newspaper clippings and tracked down certain individuals. Many of them refused to see me (including the famous writer Karina Masterson, among others), some I was successful in interviewing and here I would like to take the opportunity to personally thank them, without naming names, since all of them specifically asked that I respect their anonymity.

In any case, from what I have been able to piece together, the initial incident started one August afternoon in 1990, in Miami. It was a scorchingly hot day, the sun was melting asphalt roads and consuming everything in the sky, burning away white clouds and making sluggish old black cars even hotter, when Joe Cavallaro went into Burton's Supermarket to return an antibiotic, purchased a few days earlier, to the pharmacy, since it had been prescribed by his doctor for a strange inflammation of his jaw but the swelling went down before he was supposed to start taking the medicine.

The only problem was that the young lady at the register, a tall black woman with nostrils flaring wearing a white lab coat that accentuated her pointy tits, glared at him and told him that he couldn't return the antibiotic, let alone have his twenty-five bucks back, because there was a federal law in the state of Florida which forbade it. Joe showed her the receipt: "all merchandise may be returned within thirty days for full reimbursement". The lanky black woman, unmoved, said that the receipt referred to other merchandise, not pharmaceuticals. Joe kept his cool, because black people are pretty touchy and you need to be careful, so he pointed out to her that the receipt he had in his hand was for this specific medication, not some other merchandise, and the receipt clearly stated that he could return whatever he had bought within thirty days and be reimbursed. The black woman's nostrils flaired again and she repeated that there was a federal law standing in the way. "Can I speak with the person in charge then?" Joe Cavallaro asked. "Sure," answered the tall black woman.

The store manager, much shorter than Joe Cavallaro, had a receding hairline and was clearly pissed off. Joe explained, politely, his predicament. The store rep, rudely, said that it was a state law in Florida, no returns on prescriptions, period; Joe stressed that he was not disputing the law, but the receipt, the receipt made no reference to the federal law in Florida; the manager explained that they couldn't print different receipts for every product; Joe's response was that they needed to at least have a sign, right at the pharmacy register, informing the public that there was a no-return policy for medicine; the manager, getting more irritated with each passing second, said that *everyone else* had the same policy; Joe responded "I don't really care what *everyone else* does, *I* bought this medication here and I have a receipt that says the merchandise may be returned within thirty days and I am entitled to get my money back"; the manager again repeated that there was a federal law in Florida; Joe, exasperated, interrupted him to say, "fine, but you personally, at least, don't you think there's something a little hinky going on here?"

The manager shrugged his shoulders, stared him right in the eyes and hissed, contemptuously, "you're asking me to give you back your twenty-five bucks? My answer is NO."

Joe decided he needed to leave, otherwise he would bash the guy's face in – but then he glanced at the nametag pinned on the imbecile's shirt: "Sal Magnone, Manager." Joe looked up and stared at him, squinted, silently, his eyes now tiny slits. The rep didn't seem intimidated. Joe leaned in closer to him, slithering like a snake – the other guy stiffened as if expecting some type of threat – and he whispered into his ear, in Italian: "Sal Magnone, you don't treat a *paesano* like this."

The manager turned pale. Joe backed off, smiled pleasantly, put his left hand on the guy's right shoulder, vigorously squeezing it, and with his other hand he crumpled the nametag on the guy's chest, and, as if he were pronouncing a death sentence, this time in English he repeated: "no, Sal, you don't treat a *fellow countryman* like this…"

Sal Magnone's eyes were now wide-open, he grimaced in terror and was sweating bullets. Convulsing like an epileptic, he removed his wallet from his pants' pocket, took out twenty-five dollars, handed it, trembling, to Joe, but Joe refused to take the money, "no, Sal, there's a federal law in Florida."

"Fuck the law!"

"Sal, no need for foul language now!"

"Excuse me, sir… here's fifty dollars… a hundred…"

"Sal, now you're insulting me."

"No, sir, I beg you… *tengo famiglia*," he said in Italian.

Joe smiled paternally, took the money, patted him on the cheek, and left the store.

The second episode in Joe Cavallaro's career as a mafioso took place a couple of weeks later. I should mention that Joe Cavallaro was a Master's Degree Candidate at Atlantic Ocean University in Miami and that semester he had decided to take a course called *Postmodernist Vagina in the Fallocratic World* taught by Professor Brumilda Roquefort, a lesbian from Quebec, ugly as sin but a real academic celebrity in the States. Joe, worried about his grade on the first paper, a C+, went to see her during office hours to ask her how he had screwed up and how he could get back on the right track. So Joe was in the waiting room, in front of Roquefort's office, flipping through a magazine devoted entirely to gay Eskimo poetry, when Roquefort showed up, a half hour late. She didn't even look at him, went into her office and closed the door behind her. Joe was flabbergasted, he was in the middle of reading a sonnet about two Inuit males (whose love-making was interrupted by a monk seal), he stopped reading and knocked timidly on the door. He heard a grunt. He bravely braced himself, went into the office and sat down in front of Roquefort's desk while she sat opposite him cheerfully chatting on the phone, not coming down off her high horse to even acknowledge him.

Finally Roquefort ended her phone conversation with a bois-terous belly laugh, turned to Joe, and from behind her thick glasses said, "what can I do for you?"

"It's... it's about my *paper*..."

"Spit it out, I don't have all afternoon, what do you want to know?"

"Well, I would like to know what I did wrong, so I may avoid any similar mistakes on the next..."

"Ah, well" and she laughed, but it was really a whinnying sound, like a young mare, seething with rage and delight, "if you don't understand what's wrong, Mr. Cavallaro, I'm afraid there's not much hope for you."

Joe thought this was a bitter pill to swallow but realized this was the price he had to pay for being a heterosexual male, and went on humbly, "yes, of course, but you see, every professor wants something different, you gave me a C+ without any expla-nation, no remarks and..."

"I don't have the time to comment on all the bullshit that my students hand in. You are a Master's candidate, not some rookie fresh out of high school, actually it baffles me that the university would even accept someone like you into the program!"

Joe was down for the count, pummeled by a series of cruel punches, by the blind violence of his opponent, he suddenly had the feeling he was being bombarded with blows, lacerated all over his body by her arrows of humiliation. He was completely bowled over, speechless, stunned, almost in a trance, to the point that he was watching the mouth of this person moving, continuing to insult him, patently, but he no longer heard anything – at least until he saw her laughing so hard she nearly fell over backwards off her chair, and his hearing came back again because that equine laughter revived him, piercing his eardrums, and a hatred entirely pervaded him, a ferocious hostility, he wanted to grab her by the neck, stuff that laughter down her throat, rip her eyes out of their sockets, annihilate her. Instead he said only this: "you shouldn't talk to me like that, Professor Roquefort" – but he said it with a decidedly Italian/American accent, obviously Sicilian.

Roquefort's laughter abruptly stopped. There was a moment of silence. Joe said nothing, but he crossed his legs and cupped his hands over his face, totally concealing it, then curled his index and middle fingers under to expose only his eyes.

Professor Roquefort was completely floored, she smiled, but gone was her dismissive haughtiness, Joe realized this and he continued to remain silent, staring at her, his fingers creating fleshy bars imprisoning his eyes. There is nothing as terrifying as silence for someone who has been maligned by pernicious doubt. Professor Roquefort murmured, "I believe that our meeting is over."

Joe remained silent, let his hands fall from his face and smiled, pleasantly, enigmatically. Then, in a very deep, gruff voice, accentuated by the same tender and ominous timbre of a funeral dirge, muttered, "I too believe our little chat is over, Professor Roquefort."

He got up and left. For the rest of the semester he did not utter a single word in her class, just saying hello to Roquefort at the beginning of class and goodbye at the end, and when he would by chance bump into her in the hallways of the university he

would just say, "Professor Roquefort," ceremoniously, supercili-
ously, but always staring her down, sometimes gnawing on the
nail of his right pinky (on which he was now wearing a large gold
ring).

Joe got an *A* on the remaining papers and passed the course
with flying colors.

The third part of this story, at least according to the records
of the lawsuit, happened on Deerfield Beach. Joe Cavallaro and
Karina Masterson were lying on the beach, not far from the tran-
quil and expansive ocean, under a huge, scarlet moon. They had
wandered down to the shoreline during a party held at the house
of the Creative Writing professor, Milton Payne, and Joe was
starting to feel a bit sick. Too much California Zinfandel, perhaps, or too many shrimp dunked into the tabasco-flavored salsa.
Or, quite simply, it was because of that idiot Karina. They had
met each other in Payne's course, which Joe Cavallaro – not having any realistic creative aspirations – attended due to the great
number of female students who were enrolled in the class (the
same reason, noted in the trial transcripts, for which he had
signed up for the *Postmodern Vagina in the Fallocratic World*
course). Karina wanted to write novels, exactly like everyone else,
and she already considered herself a writer, even though she had
never published anything, exactly like everyone else, except Professor Payne, whose Ph.D. was in creative writing and who had
published a handful of short stories in several run-of-the-mill
East Coast journals. Writers got on Joe Cavallaro's nerves, and
Karina was possibly the most nerve-racking of them all – but she
was a knock-out. Blond curls cascaded around her neck, blue
eyes the color of the Florida sky in January and February, delicate
lips painted the color of fire, breasts, thighs, she had at all.

They had gone out together for the first time with the rest of
the group, which included Milton Payne, after class, to some
kind of Irish pub on Lincoln Road, and they had talked about
Derek Walcott's poetry while downing rivers of beer, then some

of them went outside to have a smoke, others stayed to play pool. Joe – who didn't drink beer, didn't smoke, didn't play pool and least of all didn't know who the hell Derek Walcott was – had spent the entire evening nodding in agreement and pretending to laugh approvingly, but in reality he was very focused on Karina Masterson's incredible tits. She had silky blonde hair and was also wearing a pair of delicate round glasses that made her look, if it were possible, even more sexy, and, as she was babbling, she latched onto Milton Payne, her silly laughter sounding like the jingling of gold coins, showering him with whiffs of her perfume, veiled messages, fantastic tits. However, sometimes she caught the rapacious look in Joe Cavallaro's eyes, but she didn't seem to be too put off by it.

So, the following week, Joe invited her out for a drink, just the two of them this time, and Karina – surprisingly – accepted. The Miami night was delightful, a light breeze gently caressed the palm trees, the stars were twinkling and Karina's breasts, as always, rose to the occasion. They went to a sushi bar, with subdued lighting and sake, Karina talked and talked, it was basically a gossip fest about the rest of the class, and Joe loved gossip, he avidly imbibed every little acrimonious remark that tumbled out of those crimson lips, picking at raw salmon in soy sauce while surreptitiously worming his way into Karina's smugness, giving her plenty of rope with plenty of succulent bait (such as pointing out the physical defects of such and such girl or that guy's lack of writing talent) and they laughed about it and everything seemed to be leading up to an inevitable conclusion. But then Karina, who knows why, changed the subject, starting to talk about the contribution of Chilean intellectuals to democracy, and Joe could no longer keep his finger on the pulse of the discussion, wasn't able to jump in with a comment, so he feigned a concerned expression and meticulously avoided looking directly at Karina's stunning tits, because you couldn't be drooling over the tits of a person who was going on about some Chilean intellectuals' contribution to democracy. He paid the check (pretty steep) and brought her home, Karina didn't let up for a second, still enthusiastically talking about the Chilean question, and Joe was wondering how he could slip at least one sensual kiss into a conversation about Pinochet's downfall. Karina Masterson's lecture concluded on her doorstep without Joe being able to figure that out, even though he had racked his brain trying.

The party at Milton Payne's beach house was the following week. The moon was floating in the deep blue of the night sky and Karina looked amazing without going overboard: pink sneakers, a long gypsy skirt and t-shirt of the same color, her subtle makeup giving the illusion that she wasn't wearing any. Like a true star, she was firmly at the helm navigating the evening, sauntering around Milton Payne, ingratiating herself to his wife by asking for recipes and advice on decorating, dividing her time equally between the other professors at the party, scientifically methodical in not coming across as a threat to the other women and letting the slit in her skirt reveal her adorable thighs to the men. A genius, thought Joe Cavallaro, whose only pursuit the entire evening had been pouring Zinfandel into plastic glasses for himself, wolfing down jumbo shrimp and staring at Professor Roquefort (raising his glass as if toasting her and then drinking the wine with his pinky, adorned with the gold ring, raised in the air). Toward the end of the party, when the majority of guests had gone, Joe was standing by the wooden banister of a staircase, which overlooked the ocean, and was gazing at that incredible moon which had sunk into the sky like a fat Persian queen. He sensed the presence of someone nearby him, ethereal, and perfume that made him think of cold sake and Chilean intellectuals. Karina Masterson. "Take me away from this bunch of imbeciles," she whispered in Joe Cavallaro's ear. And Joe Cavallaro didn't need to be asked twice.

So they ended up on the beach, walking by the water's edge which glowed in the moonlight. At a certain point Karina sighed, histrionically, "I hate them, they're all so pathetic…."

"Who?"

"Them, all of them, with all their petty dreams, their petty convictions…"

"Yup."

"And Payne. *He's such a loser.*"

"True."

It seemed like the moonlight had made her tits bigger. As if by some type of magic Karina turned, and staring Joe in the eyes, passionately, she whispered, "is it okay with you if we sit down on the sand and look at the ocean?"

"Hell yeah, I'd really like that."

They sat down on the soft sand, and Joe Cavallaro, overwhelmed by the power of the moon and that perfume of hers (vanilla, milky, something remote he couldn't put his finger on) he caressed Karina's velvety arm and felt it vibrate like a violin, and was ready to grab hold of it, nibble on it, when she started up again on the Chilean question. Joe Cavallaro felt exasperated, was almost ready to throw in the towel, "Karina" said Joe "I'm Italian…."

"I know…."

"Well, you do understand what that means, don't you?"

"What does it mean?"

"That you don't let yourself be led down to a beach by an Italian without any tactile reaction from him. You don't drone on to an Italian about Pinochet, on the beach, wearing a strapless bra, with the most tantalizing legs I've ever seen. No, with an Italian, this is not what you do. With a Chilean, maybe. With Derek Walcott, maybe."

She looked at him, her eyes were wide-open with an indefinable expression, her mouth slightly open as if she were out of breath and you had to coax the breath out of her. Then they rolled around in the sand and the rest is history.

Joe's trial began on July 24, 1999. The courtroom in the Miami Courthouse was packed with crowds and photographers. Appearing before the court, the accused, Joe Cavallaro, had to defend himself against a charge of Mafia-style threats and criminal conspiracy entered by Joseph Goldberg, represented by his lawyer Adam Ruthenberg. The facts of the case were fairly straightforward, dating back to about a year earlier: Cavallaro had sold his old black Mustang to Goldberg, who in turn came to see Joe a month later to return the car, demanding Joe refund his money, since the engine had burnt out. Cavallaro's answer was that the car was working just fine when he had sold it to him, Goldberg – surely over eighty years old – said that "a Mustang is not okay if the engine burns out at 120 miles an hour." Amused, Cavallaro looked at the old grandpa, then said, "I'm sorry, you test drove the car, it performed beautifully."

The old guy gritted his teeth and hissed, "do you think you can fuck me over just because I'm old?"

Cavallaro started to feel exhausted, "no, absolutely not, no one is getting fucked over, sir."

"Do you think you can fuck me over just because I'm Jewish?"

And suddenly the old man went after Joe and grabbed him by the neck, Joe was dumbfounded feeling those gnarly hands choking him and inhaling his rotten-smelling breath, then he snapped out of his shock, removed the old man's hands and wanted to deck him, but the old guy screamed, "fuckin' guinea!"

Joe stared at him, right into those sky blue bloodshot eyes, and angrily snarled, "well, just remember, before you come back here again with that wreck, that I'm Italian."

"Are you threatening me? Hey, are you threatening me???" The old geezer screamed, convulsing with anger.

The matter could have been resolved easily enough, but Ruthenberg, feeling strongly that this was the case of a lifetime, had painstakingly dug into Joe's past and found at least twenty people, whom Ruthenberg reassured as a lawyer that Cavallaro had no ties to the Mafia, that were ready to testify they had received Mafia-style threats from Joe. The accusations of the witnesses were inflammatory and circumstantial, especially those made by the manager of Burton's. Sal Magnone, bald by that time, had explicitly asked for restitution of the hundred dollars (plus interest) that Cavallaro had extorted from him. But Cavallaro's lawyer, Thomas Acquadirosa, had built his entire defense on this point of contention: there was no proof that Cavallaro had any ties to the Mafia – his police record was spotless, his name had never been implicated in any shady dealings, he had an honorable academic career. "Have you ever seen, ladies and gentlemen of the jury, an academic Mafioso? Have you ever seen such a superbly refined command of the language, as demonstrated by the accused here present Joseph Cavallaro, by a Mafioso? The television and movie industries have taught us no, ladies and gentleman, and do you want to know why? Because it would not be realistic. Because the trafficking of arms and drugs is not only more profitable than any university job, but it also requires work and a full-time commitment. A Mafioso does not have time for a Ph.D!"

Then Ruthenberg pointed out that this would be palatable if Cavallaro's career had not actually relied on Mafiosi methods to achieve it, and called as his first witness Professor Brumilda Roquefort, who ferociously railed against the defendant, accusing him of having tied her to a chair in her office and threatening her by holding a knife to her throat if she didn't give him the highest mark on his final exam. The jury was visibly struck by these inflammatory statements, but Acquadirosa, in the most subtle manner, asked her the name of her course that Cavallaro was enrolled in and, in the face of Roquefort's abrupt response, *Postmodernist Vagina in the Fallocratic World*, the jury, made up of heterosexual men and women who were evangelical born-again Christians, started to look at Roquefort with a more suspect eye. Roquefort, red faced, unleashed her fury like Medusa and proceeded to detail one accusation after another, each more damaging, until she finally exploded, "and he sexually molested me!"

At this remark the whole courtroom erupted in resounding laughter, Judge de Piscopo fell off his chair, Ruthenberg put his hand on his forehead and any doubts the jury might have had concerning the validity of any of the accusations – vanished.

So, concluded Acquadirosa, how can you be threatened Mafia-style by someone who is not in the Mafia?

The jury reached a verdict. Joe Cavallaro was found not guilty.

Nine months later, there was a second trial. The Florida humidity was infernal, you couldn't breathe. The sweltering streets of Miami were oozing heat and smog, the rank smell of Cuban cigars hung in the air. All the witnesses from the first trial except Professor Roquefort (who was under investigation for perjury at the first trial) consisted of the aggrieved parties against Joe Cavallaro: accused, this time, of "fraud and damaging the welfare of a naively gullible public."

Ruthenberg based his prosecution on the fact that Cavallaro, even though he didn't belong to any crime family, behaving as if he did, had capitalized on this and generated fraudulent earnings by creating or instilling indiscriminate fear in his victims.

The witnesses repeated more or less what they had testified to at the first trial, and they cited certain gestures, looks and words with which Cavallaro, in speaking with them, had coerced them to do as he said. But they had sworn on the Bible, and no one denied under cross-examination by Acquadirosa that Cavallaro had never mentioned, in any of the incriminating conversations, any word that expressly sounded like a threat, much less the word Mafia. Cavallaro had always just confined his remarks to stating that he was Italian, as evidenced by his voice, his facial expressions and his body language. Can you consider my client guilty for stating his Italian background? Acquadirosa addressed Judge de Piscopo by postulating this observation as a rhetorical question. If asserting one's Italian heritage is synonymous with being a Mafioso, and if the result of certain expressions and gestures of someone who avers that he is Italian is misconstrued as his being a Mafioso – Acquadirosa solemnly concluded – is the blame for this attributable to my client or to someone who judges other people by relying on stereotypes and racial prejudice?

And here Acquadirosa launched into a marvelous historical-philosophical diatribe, dating back to the Mayflower and Ellis Island, combining concepts of the melting pot and tolerance, coloring his oration with such exquisite words as Liberty, Opportunity and Dreams (which caused several members of the public to take out their handkerchiefs) and since there were a couple of people on the jury with almond shaped eyes, a black man, and a freckled faced redheaded woman, he did not forget to mention that our great country, America, was built with the blood and sweat of everyone, whether Japanese, Black or Irish.

Joe Cavallaro was acquitted on all charges of fraud and damaging the welfare of a naively gullible public.

A year later, on September 15, 2000, the third and final phase of legal proceedings brought against Joe Cavallaro began. The Miami heat was stifling, even though there was no sun, the sky was stained yellow like an old smoker's teeth, and Joe Cavallaro had to answer to the toughest set of charges, rape, in a lawsuit filed by Ms. Karina Masterson. According to Masterson, Cavallaro had forcefully dragged her down to the beach and, couched in Mafia-style threats, coerced her to have sexual intercourse with him. "Why didn't you ever mention this before?" Asked a pack of journalists, who had mobbed the bronze front door of her sumptuous Key Biscayne villa early one morning, "I was afraid," sighed Karina, her eyes ringed with tears, dressed in a white Calvin Klein terry cloth robe, but a journalist wearing a green scarf on her head pounced on her, "but Cavallaro's first trial established that he's not in the Mafia," "I was ashamed," and Karina ended any further dialogue with the reporters, putting her hand on her forehead mimicking the Italian actress Eleonora Duse, and went back into her house.

Masterson's denunciation exploded thunderously beyond the state of Florida, it was in the papers and on TV all over America, the end result being that all the most famous editors, who had initially declined to publish her novel, were now suddenly interested in her work, and Karina Masterson was a guest on all the *in* talk shows, she shed crocodile tears and let herself be comforted by the popular TV host Evelyn Stubbon, who hugged Karina in a sign of solidarity.

Things had become pretty tough for Joe Cavallaro, but Acquadirosa never lost his cool even for a minute. Ascertaining what had exactly happened on that beach was next to impossible, it was a case of *he said, she said*, but in the end the truth wasn't important. It was a morality trial, and it would play out as a moral judgment call not only for the jury but for the entire country as well.

Ruthenberg's invective was unrelenting, Masterson became not only the sacrificial victim of Cavallaro's violent rapaciousness but the symbol of the exploited female gender archetype, enslaved, raped by the male of the species, and America once again, through that trial, would be able to trailblaze a path toward sexual equality and a new society. "My client is a woman, there's no denying it, correct?" And everyone, jury, judge and journalist, turned toward Karina who, coached by her lawyer, lowered her face demurely. "I ask you, ladies and gentlemen of the jury, should she have to pay for this? Does the fact that she's a woman give any coward the right to impose himself on her with force and deception?" The women of the jury could appreciate this, while the men registered no emotion. It was an all-white jury and they appeared to be upright Americans from different generations, so her lawyer further stoked the fire and improvised with a new metaphor, describing Karina Masterson as America herself, generous and kind, one who gives a chance to anyone coming from whatever part of the world who asks her for that chance, but is then betrayed, raped and stabbed in the back by those same people whom she had welcomed as her children.

The metaphor hit home, the public murmured its approval, the jurors were visibly moved by such poetic images, and it was now Acquadirosa's turn to speak and he was brutally honest in asking the jurors: "can Ms. Masterson be considered the poster child for the female gender?" Everyone turned once again to stare at Masterson, who was not expecting this and she instinctively stuck out her chest, letting her dazzling smile electrify the jury, and she beamed broadly, which was as marvelous as it was captivating. As much as Ruthenberg had implored her to keep a low profile, maybe to even look a little sloppy, and to tone down her beauty as much as possible, Karina Masterson oozed sensuality from every pore. No one could forget, while she was hugging the popular TV host Evelyn Stubbon, the way the risqué slit in her fuchsia skirt had opened up like a Norwegian fjord, or the unbridled sensuality of her breasts and her burgundy colored lips while she sighed repeatedly telling her tear jerking story to Evelyn and the public, both deeply distressed.

Now, Acquadirosa knew something about human beings and their vanity. His colleague Ruthenberg believed that whites hated blacks, that men hated women and that everyone hated Jews, but Acquadirosa also actually understood a more categorical side of the real world: that women hate other women, especially if they're beautiful, and that writers hate other writers, especially if they're successful. Acquadirosa tracked down Professor Milton Payne, the creative writing teacher, as well as several former classmates of Karina Masterson. Acquadirosa informed them that a wealthy New York publisher, sensing the increasing interest in the persona of Karina Masterson as auspicious, had optioned her first novel, sight unseen.

"That bitch," said Erica Gustaffsson, a buxom girl with delicate glasses who wore her red hair in a bob.

"That kiss ass," said Helena Silverstone, who had pitch-black hair and whose nose was shaped like an owl's beak.

"That whore," said Professor Payne.

Ah, writers! Thought Acquadirosa, with a satisfied smile.

Everyone agreed to testify as individuals who were well informed about the facts, and all of them, despite Ruthenberg's objections, painted Karina as ruthless, sneaky, and absolutely talentless.

"Objection! The perceptions of the witnesses are purely subjective," shouted Ruthenberg once again, and Acquadirosa countered:

"How subjective is the perception of Karina that you have presented to the court, Mr. Ruthenberg, equating her to our great country, America, and I quote verbatim, as 'generous and kind, one who gives a chance to anyone coming from whatever part of the world who asks her for that chance, but is then betrayed, raped and stabbed in the back by those same people whom she had welcomed as her children'."

The murmur of approbation resounded among the public and several jurors once again had to take out a handkerchief to dry their eyes. Ruthenberg, flattered by being quoted and egged on by the latest reaction of the courtroom audience, exclaimed, "I maintain my claim! Karina Masterson is America!"

"But, in this type of equation, we have only one constant, which is that our country is – beyond all reasonable doubt – a great country, generous and kind, one that offers an opportunity to anyone coming from whatever part of the world and asks for a chance here, but is then stabbed in the back, betrayed and raped by the same ones whom it had welcomed as sons and daughters. Or does anyone of you beg to differ?" Acquadirosa asked emphatically and no one on the jury or anybody seated in the courtroom dared contest such an evident truth. "But" Acquadirosa went on "concerning the behavior of Karina Masterson we have heard testimony, to the contrary, which is not terribly flattering: that she's materialistic, not terribly talented, guilty of plagiarism, is aggressive and is a seductress. Is this our America?"

There was a moment of total bafflement. Then Acquadirosa resumed, "I call Karina Masterson to the stand."

Karina Masterson, called to answer the accusations of her former classmates and Professor Payne, initially defended herself magnificently. She covered her eyes in order to shed her tears and painfully confessed her complete surprise upon hearing the testimony of her former classmates and Professor Payne, whom, she said, she had always been very fond of. So Acquadirosa recalled Erica Gustaffsson to the stand. Of all the witnesses she had been the one whose remarks were the most damaging and detail oriented, also offering up, as an item to be entered into evidence, a paragraph written at the time by Masterson which, in fact, clearly demonstrated that she had plagiarized Virginia Woolf. Acquadirosa put Masterson and Gustaffsson in direct confrontation. Masterson profusely expressed her affection and admiration for Gustaffsson and in a voice racked by tears she told her that she had learned the most from her and in the end she suggested that hugging her would, "also symbolically, put an end to that preposterous and centuries-old rivalry between women who, instead, should unite as allies in a sisterhood against the tyranny of the male macho pig." Neither the judge nor the male jurors particularly appreciated this outburst, but the continual objections of Ruthenberg went unheeded because the judge had not had this much fun since he used to play "odds and evens" as a boy on the streets of Brooklyn. In fact, when Gustaffsson said, "I would much rather be eaten alive by a cobra than be forced to hug you," Masterson turned purple, then bright red, then yellow, she jumped up, with fire in her eyes, and boomed in a thunderous voice, "it's more likely that you would scarf down the cobra! Because you're disgustingly obese! You fat four-eyed fool of a filthy snake! Fuck you and that frigid crow of a mortician Silverstone and that loser of an assfucker Payne and that Joe Cavallaro with his limp dick and…"

It took twenty minutes to restore order in the courtroom.

It would be nice if this absurd story had a happy ending. But, unfortunately, this is not the case. Three months later, on his front doorstep, early one morning, while he was picking up the *Sun Sentinel* newspaper, Joe Cavallaro was riddled with bullets that almost certainly came from a black car with a high-powered engine. No one saw anything, the police arrived on scene after the crowd. The papers at the time placed an enormous amount of importance on what had happened, a cold-blooded murder committed while the Miami sun shone brightly, but the South Florida sun swiftly burns up facts and burns out people, they become opaque in the end rendering them invisible, people are old and they only want to play golf during the day and go out to restaurants at night and, for this reason, with each passing day the newspaper articles dwindled to a few short paragraphs.

From what I have been able to piece together (since it wasn't easy, between the reluctance of some to speak about the matter and the sheer forgetfulness of others) the police began to explore three investigative leads that were based on three possible theories. The first: Joe Cavallaro had been killed on orders from Karina Masterson's father, a very powerful businessman with very traditional values, who had recently been elected a senator, who wanted to make Joe pay for irrevocably disgracing his daughter's reputation, as well as for the humiliation she had to endure during the trial. The second: Joe Cavallaro had been killed by orders from an influential feminist organization, inspired by the writings of the distinguished Brumilda Roquefort, who had labeled Cavallaro as the epitome of the macho man. The third: Joe Cavallaro had been killed by a syndicate of Italian/Americans lead by Judge de Piscopo, who wanted to punish Cavallaro for having contributed to reinforcing the stereotype that all Italian/Americans were Mafiosi.

Following up on even one of the three investigations would have caused an unheard of cloud of dust and yanked on chains that shouldn't be rattled. The police preferred to put the case to bed. Still waters run deep, better not to disturb them. Better to let the heat envelop the city. Better to start talking about something else again, the iguana infestation or the chihuahua eaten by the alligator. The investigation was filed away in the archives as a settling of scores between Mafia families.

A Pointed Finger

I

My friend Alfredo Crepuscolo used to go to the campus cafeteria every day, around eight, before his classes. The cafeteria is located in the heart of the campus and, aside from coffee, you can get a bit of everything: one after the other in a circle are the *Tai-Chin Asian* food concession, with its steamy aroma of grease, *Salsarita*, where lovely Guatemalan girls prepare empanadas and gazpacho, and *Mamma Leone* for paninis stuffed with meatballs, and so on.

Rosa was the manager of the *Burger King* and from behind the counter she instructed directed helped the kids she supervised, usually Blacks and South Americans: she cooked hamburgers and her face was flushed from the red hot grill and the deep fryer. Cooking and serving the students lined up at the counter wasn't, strictly speaking, her job, but she did it anyway because she enjoyed the students calling her by her first name and she enjoyed saying "have a nice day" to them. Most of the time, however, she had her back to the public like an orchestra conductor, dressed in her tight-fitting regulation blue work uniform, but she turned around from time to time and the first thing she did was glance down at the shoes of the people in line. One day, seeing Alfredo's shoes, she looked him straight in the eye and said, "you're Italian."

She used to say you could spot an Italian by the shoes he wore.

II

At that hour the campus is always deserted, more or less, small songbirds begin to warble on their branches, secretaries peruse the mail, librarians replace books used during the night back on the shelves, and students groan from rumpled beds in dormitories, smelling of oatmeal.

And so Rosa had the time to sit at a table with Alfredo. They drank coffee and looked out the large windows at the sunlight filtering through the trees or at the grass still wet from the morning rain, and they talked. Rosa had told him that she was born in Calabria, but her Italian was a unique crossroad of nuanced inflections. It wasn't so much that she anglicized a few words or that she sometimes ended her sentences using a distinctly American grammatical structure, actually her Italian was rather good and, at times, she nailed the subjunctive tenses – but sometimes she sounded oddly unnatural as she alternated between a heavy southern rhythm (especially when she was agitated) and a northern cadence (when she was describing something indifferently). One day Alfredo asked her, "where did your northern accent come from?"

She stared at him, smiling. She was still a beautiful woman. She was over fifty, a mother of three, with fleshy thighs, but had the face of a young girl. She said to him, "imagine something... imagine a stone house. Imagine seven people, each one standing next to the other."

Alfredo imagined everything, just as she had requested. She continued smiling and staring at him, she seemed to be enjoying herself, and she was biting her lower lip. Two childlike ash blond curls were poking out from beneath the cap that completely covered her hair and caressed her tiny ears, which resembled small seashells. Then she took out a pack of blue Capri cigarettes. As they did every morning, they walked across the lawn and sat at the same small wooden table under an enormous oak tree, majestically dominating the campus, to chat, finish their coffee and smoke. Alfredo is not a heavy smoker but he really savored that cigarette – the first and only one of the day – with that sense of benevolence which inspires the morning, the wide open South

Florida sky, the pleasures of coffee and of classrooms waiting for him, and the books that were expecting him.

III

"I've imagined the seven people, Rosa. Now what?"

"And how do you picture them?"

"How do I picture them?... Well, from the tallest to the shortest. The first one is a girl, very, very slim and tall..."

"No, it's a boy," she said dryly.

"But he's tall."

"He's fourteen years old. They're all looking forward, right? Like they're posing for a photograph."

"Or a line-up."

"What does that mean?"

"Like you see in police movies where somebody from behind a one-way mirror has to pick out the guilty one from a line-up of people."

Her dark eyes flashed, as if Alfredo had disclosed some disturbing detail. She removed the cigarette from her mouth, breathed in and whispered, "good... right..."

Now, that flash in her eyes, he had seen it at other times since he met her. She was a kind and generous woman, but every now and then she threw a fit, out of the blue, and unleashed a string of obscenities in Calabrian dialect. She had a dazzling smile but sometimes you sensed a tinge of melancholy, or nostalgia, something that inexplicably transported Alfredo back to his little town in Italy – those Sunday mornings, early – a resplendent spring sky as he was watering the flowers on the balcony and the ancient streets and gardens were slowly waking up, and he smelled the fragrant scent of freshly made bread and everything implied contentment and, all of a sudden, the far-off sound of a piano, in the distance, coming from who knows where, troubled him, unsettled him.

IV

The campus was still saturated from the overnight rain, the grass squished as they walked, and whatever Rosa might say, Alfredo would be fine with it. She always did most of the talking, in the time it took to smoke that cigarette, and she told him about that bastard ex-husband of hers, about her three grown children scattered all over the country, about that damned Chinaman, her boss, who was always bugging her and "didn't know shit about anything" and was twenty years younger than she. Alfredo almost always listened to her, only rarely did he get distracted by watching the frenzied scampering of a couple of squirrels or by remembering the rush of seeing a certain coed's legs, but it wasn't the case this time because Rosa had caught his attention, "hey Rosa, I don't get it: is this a game?"

Rosa blew out the last puff of smoke and gave him an indecipherable look, vacant and ironic at the same time, then said, "no, it's not a game. You asked me where my accent comes from, didn't you? I have to go now, Fred."

V

Alfredo didn't think much more about it. His classes were in the morning (he teaches art history) so he returned to the cafeteria around noon. At that hour the cafeteria is swarming with students and it's frenetic at each food concession. Rosa's face is redder than ever, she's strict but protective of her employees, and everyone picks up the pace following her orders, like members of an orchestra who blindly trust the conductor. Alfredo avoids the Burger King line but yells, "ciao, Rosa!" And she, normally with her back to the line, turns, sees his shoes, looks up and shouts back, "ciao Fred, you want something?"

He never wants anything and heads for the salad bar. Then he spends the whole afternoon in the library, wandering through the stacks, fingering the spines of books, pulling out a few, crouching like a cat between the shelves of the American Impressionists and the Pre-Raphaelites, getting lost looking at reproductions of ancient paintings or reading the biography of a forgotten artist. Sometimes he wanders over to the well-worn armchair, set in a recess in front of the full-length third floor window, and places a pile of books at the foot of the chair. Every so often he looks up from his notebook and glances outside, the space is filled with light between the parched South Florida soil and the limitless sky, the dried green dense vegetation and the stark white of the low houses scorched by the sun, the aquamarine flecks of swimming pools and the pink pastels of the mansions, and Alfredo's gaze gets lost and it drifts farther still, follows the horizon and reaches the ocean, crosses over the large black ocean, a tempestuous ocean, inhabited by sea monsters and the ghosts of sailors, whales and shipwrecks, but his gaze soars and continues on, reaching the shores of Spain, yellow, raw umber Spain, the red tinged Spain of Picasso, and then it flies, flies over France, blue and gray France, the France of dancers and prostitutes, and then finally over Italy, his Italy. He enters through a tiny window, the lights are on and he sees his mother cooking a meat sauce, he looks at her eyes and a single tear is sliding down her cheek and Alfredo touches his own cheek feeling that tear and thinks, "damn, what good eyesight I have!"

VI

The next morning, hot and sun-drenched, felt like a June morning – but it was November. The word November sounds frigid, harsh, even morose, but not in South Florida. The venerable senior citizens of South Florida don't give a damn about November or death, they don't give a damn about anything, they wear small orange hats and short blue skirts, gorge themselves on chocolate cake and smoke Cuban cigars. On Saturday nights they tip the valet who parks the Porsche nicely, eat to their heart's content in Mizner Park's most expensive restaurants, go to clubs, dance until dawn and the next day they still look vibrant, ready for a day of suntan oil, rare steaks and tennis. Although tanned and dressed like teenagers, even they are bent over and have varicose veins, even they use canes and have hacking coughs, but they don't give a damn, not about their sciatica or their rheumatism, not about the weather or nostalgia, not about November and death. Sometimes they're charming and pleasant, at other times obnoxious and ridiculous, but the old folks in South Florida are unique in the world and no one quite knows why. Maybe because they live so close to an ocean that's constantly changing colors, maybe because they have worked all their lives and now they only want to enjoy themselves, maybe because they get lost in their huge houses flooded with tropical sunshine, surrounded by precious objects, very old paintings and Peruvian maids, or maybe it's simply because of the sun. The sun shines everywhere, hungry for the land, it burns brightly on the soft green of the golf courses, on the asphalt of Ocean Boulevard, on the bristly tops of the pine trees, on the mango branches where iguanas calmly bask in its heat, on the palm fronds and on the wild orchids in the lush gardens, and on the dark skin of the gardeners.

Rosa, picking up the thread of their conversation from where she had stopped, as if five minutes had passed and not twenty-four hours, asked Alfredo, "so, did you understand who the seven people are?"

"I don't know who six out of the seven are, but the seventh one is you."

"Very good!" She lit up, magically.

"Thank you, thanks. And then what?"

"And then you have to tell me. What are they doing?"

"They're looking, they're looking straight ahead..."

"And who are they looking at?"

"I don't know. But they're smiling..."

Alfredo is an optimist by nature. Rosa let her cigarette burn, suspended in the air, and once again she assumed that vacant expression, ironic or perhaps sad, "yes, they're smiling. But only for a short time."

VII

The whole thing began to intrigue him. Where was Rosa going with this? And why didn't she just tell him everything straight out?

Alfredo is a casual reader of mysteries. Especially Agatha Christie, Georges Simenon, and Nero Wolfe. Their stories are not action-packed mysteries, Alfredo is lazy and even the physical activity of others wears him out. Like most mystery readers, he told me when we had gone fishing one evening, the final resolution of the crime is the least important detail: "not that I'm not curious to find out who's guilty, but you know how it is, the discovery always verges on disappointment and the destination is less exciting when you reach it than when you're pursuing it. No, in the murder mysteries I like those little warm things, as relaxing and reassuring as a blanket on a cold winter night: Miss Marple's good manners, how proudly Poirot grooms his mustache and his irritation each time people take him for a Frenchman, the conversations between Maigret and his wife, Nero Wolfe's protruding belly and his misanthropy."

We didn't catch even one fish and we chatted like we usually did but he, even though I didn't know about it yet, he was still thinking about seven people and a house... the house! He had forgotten about the house! He had concentrated on the seven people and had completely forgotten about the house! Poirot would never have been as careless as this, or if he had, once he remembered, he would have assembled all the suspects in a room, smoothed down his mustache with a flourish, and would have rattled the truth off point by point.

VIII

"The house, Rosa, what type of house was it?"

"A stone house."

"Stone? So made of stone?"

"Didn't I say that?"

"In southern Italy?"

"Yes."

"Calabria?"

"Yes."

"The other six are your brothers and sisters?"

"Yes."

"What are they looking at?"

"Well, what they're looking at, Fred..." she whispered it, while the cigarette quickly burned down to the filter.

"Why are they smiling and suddenly they're no longer smiling?"

"Oh, Fred, you don't want to know!"

"*What do you mean* I don't want to know?"

"It's a harrowing story, Fred."

Rosa looked down, toward the lawn, blew out a puff of smoke that seemed angry, then she got up, like she was pushed forward by a spring, to go back to work. Alfredo felt slightly embarrassed and he didn't even have a mustache to slick down, so he got up and followed her cautiously, and they crossed the sun-drenched lawn without saying a word and went back to the cafeteria. Usually, at the door he said goodbye to her and left, but this time he went in with her and accompanied her all the way to the Burger King counter. He was afraid that she had changed her mind, since her mood swings made her edgy, and Alfredo would not have been surprised if she had suddenly decided to pull him off the investigation, as the cops would say. She was already behind the counter inspecting the grills and putting away utensils, moving large containers of Coke and marking off the checklists which were on large blocks of paper near the hot dog rotisserie, as she smiled and gave orders to her musicians – while he was still standing on the opposite side of the counter, pretending to be interested in the day glow menu above the griddle where they were still frying bacon & eggs.

"Want something, Fred?" He heard her say, but she meant something to eat.

"No, I'll be eating way too much on Thanksgiving, see ya Rosa," he answered, since it seemed clear to him that there wouldn't be any time for additional questions and that he would have to postpone his interrogation until the day after Thanksgiving – shit! He was forever forgetting important details: the following day the university would be closed because of the Thanksgiving festivities and so Alfredo would have to wait until Monday to continue their conversation.

"Rosa!"

She turned around. Alfredo looked at her and said, "What do you think about us having dinner together? At that Chinese buffet you told me about, near your house... it's on me, obviously."

Rosa lit up with a beaming smile, a coquettish light gleaming in her eyes, but she knew that Alfredo had no ulterior motive in inviting her out:

"Not tonight. Tonight I'm going to visit Jeffrey and Lisa. But I'll be back tomorrow, how's tomorrow night?"

Jeffrey and Lisa were her old aunt and uncle in Fort Myers whom she often visited.

"Okay, tomorrow at six-thirty. Get all dolled up."

"Ooh! My first date in ten years!" And she went back to the grills, smiling.

IX

The Chinese buffet had good choices that would satisfy any appetite and it wasn't expensive: a fixed price menu, all you could eat, not even fifteen bucks. The decor was bare bones, a series of little black tables engraved in gold and love seats the color of porcelain jade dragons, and on the wall a poster of the Great Wall. In the center of the room was a very long appealing buffet table with dozens of very hot chafing dishes full of meat and fish, enormous soup tureens and trays of desserts which you piled on your plate with little stainless steel tongs, while graceful waitresses with mother-of-pearl features served iced tea and stirred up memories of nights that never existed in old Shanghai.

Excited by the spicy vapors wafting through the room, Alfredo and Rosa scoped out the dishes on their first stroll around the buffet, picking prudently so they could come back a second, maybe even a third time (the first time around was always the most dangerous, since you tended to overdo it). Alfredo helped himself to a large piece of grilled salmon, dripping in sauce, and, clearly, took too many fried vegetables, while Rosa filled a bowl with spicy soup, morsels of pork floating in it, and she took some bamboo shoot salad as well. They went back to their table quite satisfied and, after a while, his mouth full of food, he tackled the question, "Rosa, I don't understand a lot of your story."

"Tell me about it!"

"What do you mean?"

"That even I learned the story like this, like you, through images.... How can I explain it?"

"Just try." (Christ, these Chinese know how to cook!)

Rosa was sipping the soup, searching for the words, "successive images. One after the other. And I pieced them together. Slowly. My head ached, day and night, for years…"

"But why? This is your story! *You* were one of the seven people lined up…"

Then he stopped, all of a sudden, smacking himself on the forehead, "you were a child!"

"Exactly, Fred, I was a child, didn't I tell you that? I was three years old, it was '53 or '54. I'm going for more food, you coming?"

His plate was still half-filled with vegetables, but he couldn't let her out of his sight. They got up and walked around the buffet again. Alfredo grabbed some orange chicken, while he watched his friend study the food, her maternal thighs snug in her black dress pants, a white blouse with puffy sleeves. Suddenly, in a voice that sounded uncharacteristically cold, Alfredo asked her, "were your father and mother in the room?"

Delicately bending over a tray of tofu, with a steaming dish in her hand, she turned around. She wasn't smiling. For a moment Alfredo was ashamed of his persistence, then he heard her say in a faint voice, "of course they were there."

What scheme had those two country bumpkins concocted!?

X

The evening was warm and the sky was one of those mystical skies, so typical of the tropics, a whole gamut of blues veined with gold and cardinal red from the last rays of the sun.

"Will you come to my house for coffee?" Rosa asked him. Alfredo knew that, more than having coffee, it meant a lot to her to show him her apartment, which she was very proud of, because she had earned it by scraping by, through the sweat of her brow making French fries and handing out hamburgers.

The apartment wasn't really spacious, but comfortable. As soon as you came in, a large wooden Madonna welcomed you into the small living room, which was connected to and at the same time separated from the minuscule kitchen by a low wall, almost three feet tall, like a bar counter. She hurried into the tiny kitchen to make coffee while Alfredo made himself at home on the comfortable sofa, in front of a television that was too large, and he listened absent-mindedly as Rosa described – enthusiastically – the negotiations that dragged on before she could buy the apartment, relishing the bureaucratic details, precisely stating costs, interest rates, mortgages and the problems with the real estate market which didn't interest him in the least. Alfredo looked around: the room was full of photos and holy pictures, they filled every bit of free space, mass cards and silver frames, on bookshelves, on the small dividing wall, even on top of the enormous TV and on a pile of DVDs. He got up and began to look closely at the photos (Rosa was explaining the advantages of hurricane insurance). Photos, photos and more photos. Especially of children, of her children Salvatore, Joseph and Tommasina, and of cousins and uncles at weddings, Communions, Confirmations. There were photos in black and white, others in the lively and sad colors of the '70s. Rosa served the coffee (very strong, it would probably keep him up for three days straight) meanwhile she continued talking, even about the value of the dollar. But with so many photos it was difficult to pick out her mother and father, Alfredo was tempted to ask her but Rosa went back to the kitchen to clean the coffee pot and continued to flit from one topic to another which had nothing to do with her family. Then, mixed in with the others, Alfredo saw the photo of a tiny boy. Two, three years max. He was emaciated, with large black circles under his eyes, and he appeared to have Down syndrome. But he was looking into the camera, and now he was looking at him, his mouth barely open and the look in his eyes veiled by a kind of stupor, or confusion, like a small animal, oblivious, trying to communicate something to you, that he's afraid, perhaps, or just happy that you're there.

"This is Nicola. My angel." Rosa had moved next to Alfredo without him realizing it. Silence. Then he heard her say, "Nicola was born with a lot of problems. He was in the hospital for three years and never came home. I went to the hospital every day for three years. Then God called him to Heaven. He was my first child."

It gave Alfredo goose bumps. But Rosa was calm as she sipped her coffee. She caressed the photo with a faint smile, imperceptibly, but it seemed to encompass all the tenderness of every mother in the world, that extraordinary, unique feeling, and a stream of images of *Madonna and Child* paintings paraded through his head. Then she said, "and to think that his bastard of a father never wanted to see him."

"What a piece of shit!" Alfredo blurted out so indignantly it surprised even him.

"Hey Fred, watch you language…"

He looked at her flabbergasted, "but, Rosa…"

"He's still the father of my children. Only I can call him a piece of shit. What a piece of shit!"

XI

Alfredo took a chance, "do you have any pictures of your husband?"

She got up and came back with a large cream-colored book, a photo album. They both got comfortable on the sofa, close to one another, and started to flip through it.

"Here he is," and she pointed to a puny little man, with a Sicilian mustache.

"He's very small," said Alfredo.

"Yes, but his hands were big."

"You mean that…"

"He used to beat us. Me, and my children. You didn't dare contradict him or question his authority. But you pay for everything in this life, Fred. I lost a son because God wanted it that way, he lost three children because that's what *he* wanted."

"What do you mean?"

"My daughter Tommasina was sixteen years old when, one day, she found him screwing the secretary, on the desk in his office. And to think that then he married her, that slut! With her fake tits, can you believe it, what is it with you men that you all like that stuff?"

"Who knows? Then what happened?"

"And then my daughter comes home, screaming like a maniac, bolts into her room, locks herself in, meanwhile her brothers and I don't understand a thing… and then her father comes home, Tommasina comes out, like a monster from hell, Fred, I will never forget it, her eyes were burning like two flames and she pokes him with her finger and…" She remained silent for a second, almost reliving the scene. Then she continued, "and she accuses him in front of all of us and do you know what happens next? He denies it! He says she's crazy, that her mind is playing tricks on her, that she invented everything to make him look bad in my eyes, so she flung herself against him, then I got between them and, needless to say, he was getting ready to whack me with the back of his hand, but then Salvatore, my oldest, grabs his wrist, already in mid-air, and he puts himself between us and says, if you touch Mom one more time, I'll kill you."

"Good for him!"

"He left that same day and since then the children have never wanted to see him again, end of story. Salvatore didn't even want to invite him to his wedding, *I* had to convince him to."

"But why?"

"Because he's still his father, don't you see? No, you don't get it. A father has to go to his son's wedding. If only to stop people from gossiping, plus you don't want to embarrass the bride's family... Anyway, he came and stayed in a corner the whole time and no one spoke to him. Look here."

She pointed to a photo taken at her son's wedding, there he was, a cocky smile on his puss, immortalized in an absurd pose.

"But what was he doing?" Asked Alfredo.

"He was dancing. Dancing all by himself."

XII

Rosa got up and offered him more coffee. But he passed, his nerves were already as jumpy as grasshoppers. Then she went to the kitchen and, from a cupboard with a picture of Saint Anthony on it, she pulled out a bottle of Wild Turkey and two glasses, then filled them to the brim. Alfredo could have done without the booze, but he wanted to get to the bottom of her family saga, so he got up from the sofa and sat on the tall stool in front of the little wall/counter where Rosa had placed the glasses and the bottle. So, with him on one side of the little wall and her on the other, she seemed like a young lush who stays up all night listening to the bar stories of a middle-aged bartender who's seen it all and nothing phases him anymore. After the first swig of whiskey, Alfredo asked her, "but, Rosa, how could you stay with that guy for such a long time?"

"Who knows, Fred? If I married him, there was once something endearing about him. Besides, marriage is a serious thing, Fred, a promise before God. We had three children. I have to say that we never wanted for anything, he's the kind of guy who works really hard, now you just see this apartment but we used to live in a four-bedroom house with a pool. You know, maybe it's not big enough for you, but you've never been poor, and if you've never been poor you don't know what being destitute means, if you haven't walked in my shoes… "

"I'm sorry, but there's something I don't understand. From what little I know about the marriage laws here in Florida, aren't you entitled to half of his assets in the divorce settlement? Or at least a sizeable alimony?"

"Sure. But I never wanted a penny from that pig."

Alfredo was dumbfounded, he couldn't believe his ears.

"Sorry, I don't get it."

"Oh, Fred, Fred, I know you can't understand it, even my kids didn't understand, nor did my lawyer, nobody understands… but it was a question of my *dignity*."

"But… but excuse me Rosa, you turned down a pile of money and you bust your behind twelve hours a day and…" He was going to say, "you live in a crappy apartment," luckily he caught himself, meanwhile she came back with, "but *I have* my dignity. I have my *honor*." She articulated her words proudly, as if she were pleading her case before a jury ready to convict her.

"But do you know how happy you made him?" He was stating the obvious and he knew it, certainly her children had frantically told her, a million times, not to mention her lawyer – you pig headed Calabrian, damn you and that twisted idea of dignity or honor that they've drummed into you!

But Alfredo really couldn't get over this and *he* relished the pleasure, now thirsting for blood, of seeing that animal on his knees, wringing every last dollar out of him, sucking out his marrow, feeding on his flesh, gloating over it in the Palm Beach sun, and then he saw that thrill elude him, slip through his fingers, as he imagined the sneering, satisfied smile of such a horrible person, "You could have bled him dry for every time he slapped you, Rosa, taken away his pride, kicked him to the ground, forced him to work harder and you could have had a good life on his dime, Rosa..."

"What the fuck do I care, Alfredo?"

The harshness of her reply shook him, and for the first time she used his full name. She poured him another two fingers of whiskey and seemed to be searching inside her glass, trying to find the words to make him understand. Then she suggested going into the garden for a smoke. The night was hot and the moon glimmered on the large ferns, on the pinks and oranges of the bougainvilleas, on the yellows of the hibiscus. The smoke disappeared between the palm fronds, into the air saturated with tropical perfumes, and Rosa said, "revenge? I'm not interested in revenge, Fred. Only God can judge us, not other men. And he's the father of my children. Money certainly would have made my life comfortable, I know, I'm not an idiot. But it disgusted me to take any money from him. It disgusted me to still be dependent on him. I didn't know how to do anything, not a thing. I got married at twenty-four and started having kids. I washed and ironed and cooked, I didn't know how to do anything else. I was a slave, Fred. I no longer wanted to be a slave. When we got divorced I had to learn how to do something, I did every kind of job, I started at Burger King and cleaned the restrooms for six dollars an hour. I cleaned the johns part-time. But I also put my heart into cleaning those bathrooms part-time, Fred, because I had such rage inside me, you can't even begin to imagine. And then I started to work my way up the ladder, they put me in the kitchen, then at the cash register, then they started giving me more responsibilities, I took the management test, they made me assistant-manager, and now I'm the manager and seven people work for me and I make $45,000 a year. And this is why I'm very happy with this apartment even though it's so small. *I* earned it, you see, through *my* perseverance, because of *my* courage. Sure, I work my ass off but I hold my head up high."

XIII

"But Rosa was right about one thing," Alfredo told me, "I've never known what being destitute is and life has always been good to me."

In fact, Alfredo's parents were neither rich nor poor: they were both teachers who had raised him so that he never wanted for anything nor felt the need to want more than he had. He spent a carefree adolescence bouncing between girls and soccer matches and the magical discovery of art, he was a decent student, nothing exceptional, first in high school and then in college, hampered by his indolence but morally pushed by the fact that his parents were footing the bill for his education. Then, when life was about to present him with the gruesome prospect of taking useless competitive exams to get a spot on a job placement list, of begging even for a dozen or so days off and of becoming another little monster integrated into society, a year before graduation he won a scholarship to finish his courses and write his thesis at Purdue University, West Lafayette, Indiana, USA – *America!* Truth be told, he didn't actually win: the two guys ahead of him withdrew from the competition for personal reasons – let's just say they couldn't handle being away from Mommy – so suddenly Alfredo was rushed onto a jumbo jet, his first time on a plane, enjoying the little salted crackers, watching the clouds, ecstatic, feeling like an adventurous pioneer, and relieved, since he felt that he had just barely dodged a bullet, having escaped, at the last possible moment, the monotony of daily mediocrity – he was going to America! Because in the end that was it: America. The America he had inside him since he was a boy, that he got a taste for by reading the Donald Duck and Mickey Mouse comics or watching *Happy Days*, it was like taking a drug every time anyone mentioned something typically American to him, liberty and Alabama, the cotton plantations and the Alamo, Sitting Bull and Frank Sinatra. That taste permeated him, right to the bone, it made his heart jump with joy, something he kept discovering in a film from the '40s with Tyrone Power or in the swing of Cole Porter or in F. Scott Fitzgerald's *The Great Gatsby*, when he listened to Dolly Parton's *Coat of Many Colors* on the radio, or when, enthralled, he flipped through the pages of a large book of paintings from the Hudson River School and he drank a Coke: America. But what was that taste, could Alfredo explain it, now that he had lived here in America for years and the significance of those names had lost most of their electrifying charge and Coca-Cola is only a soft drink and Alabama is only a state in the South?

It was a taste that he still associates, to this day, with the word *freedom*, and the word *freedom* means a pack of *Wrigley's,* the American gum he chewed as a boy, a wide-ranging taste, an infinite blue sky, a huge flag, its stars and stripes waving gracefully in the wind, eagles, the Old West, the prairie, bushels of corn on the cob and silos, little red mailboxes and milk bottles left by the milkman on doorsteps early in the morning, the wet sidewalks of New York and the theaters on Broadway.

That year at Purdue was very beautiful. It was like a fairy tale, immersing himself completely into a myth, seeing the wooden houses of West Lafayette where real Americans lived, talking with real Americans, hearing them say they were born in West Virginia or Wisconsin, hearing them pronounce the most enchanting names – Boston, Hemingway, bacon & eggs – with the most straightforward spontaneity. Americans! He loved Americans. Aside from the fact that he didn't think they really existed and believed they were part of his fantasy and he needed a little time to convince himself that someone could actually be a flesh and blood American, and not just a figure in a Norman Rockwell painting – Americans were all so nice. It was probably the Midwest (another marvelously evocative word) and it also probably seemed unreal to them meeting a genuine Italian, born in Italy, and not even in Sicily! But Alfredo found their kindness exquisite, they were all nice, at the market, on the street, at the university, the mailman as much as the cashier and the university President, they all said hello to you even if they had never seen you before in their lives and, what's more, they even asked you how you were. It was fantastic. A sublime civility. And out of all of them, the kindest was Professor Sciagarone, his advisor, the one who took the trouble to steer Alfredo through the back alleys and curves of bureaucratic life at an American university – as if someone could teach an Italian something on the subject.

XIV

One day, toward the end of his stay, Alfredo was in Sciagarone's office, rather depressed because his adventure was about to end. Sciagarone scrutinized him, looking up over his reading glasses, raising his head, revealing his double chin. He was truly a character taken from some old *Saturday Evening Post* cover, fat and extremely elegant, with his meticulously shined Italian black patent leather shoes, his vest with very thin yellow stripes and his bowtie, a different color every day. He was seventy-eight or even eighty or a hundred, perhaps much less, and he bragged about being Italian and even about knowing the language although it didn't go beyond a couple of Neapolitan expletives, the names of several varieties of cheese, and *O Sole Mio* (which he sang to Alfredo one evening from start to finish). He was proud that all the art in the world came from there, from *his* people, that Michelangelo, Raphael and da Vinci were all Italians, and he considered Salvator Rosa and Antonello da Messina practically his foster brothers (Sciagarone's father was from Naples and his mother from Detroit, her parents Sicilian).

"Senti, ragazzo…" he began in Italian, and after struggling with it continued in English, "they've offered me a job in Boca Raton, Florida. Head of the Art Department, something like that… I've decided to accept… you know, I'd like to learn how to play golf." He laughed crudely at his own joke (was it a joke?), so did Alfredo to make him happy. Then he began again, rearranging his reading glasses on his nose to look more professional, "among the unwritten terms of the contract, I asked if I could bring along one of my students, have him enroll in the Masters' program and make him my assistant." Alfredo grinned and, beginning to feel excited, asked, "could *I* be that student?"

"Of course, otherwise why would I be telling you all this? You must apply to the Master's in Art Program and also for an assistantship in the Art Department, this way the university will pay for almost all of the Master's degree tuition, which is very expensive, and in exchange you teach one course a semester at a very low salary, a lot lower than if they had to hire an instructor to teach these two courses. Basically, it's a *quid pro quo*, that's how it works in America."

"How low is the salary?" Alfredo asked, trembling, worried that he would still have to ask his parents for the money to cover the other three years.

"Well, very low, around $12,000 net for eight months of school. But then during the summer you would be free to teach summer courses, which are usually well paid positions, not part of the contract."

"12,000 dollars?"

"No florins."

"After thirty years of teaching my father doesn't make much more."

"Yeah, but life here is more expensive."

"I don't know about Florida, but it certainly isn't in Indiana."

He seemed to think it over, then scratched his nose and whispered softly, as if he were asking Alfredo to reveal the third secret of Fatima to him, "but how do Italians survive?"

"This is a mystery that no one has ever understood. They manage. They walk or ride bikes, because gas is very expensive. When they do drive, they go to the countryside to buy wine from farmers since it's less expensive and the quality is better. They have a remarkable instinct for avoiding impractical purchases. I do know it would be difficult for an Italian to buy a set of twenty knives, one to slice salami, one to clean fish, one to peel oranges – what I mean is, it's a beautiful thing, but one knife, that's enough, don't you think? Italians have an innate sense of a hierarchy to gauge pleasure. My father comes to mind: he loves beautiful cars, as much as the next guy, but if buying a beautiful car means he has to go into debt or even give up dinner on Friday nights in a restaurant with my mother, fuck the great car. And my mother: she's one of the most elegant women in the city, but she finds her clothes at the market at ridiculous prices and, worst-case scenario, if she doesn't find the right size or if something doesn't fit right, she alters it herself. Besides, Italians are vain, vanity is their first guilty pleasure. They would never give up having their early morning cappuccino in a luxurious café, with a view of the city, even if they have to drink coffee with chicory at home. Italians know the price of everything and the value of nothing, they are selective and don't stockpile, they choose and don't waste their money. And naturally, they don't pay their taxes."

Sciagarone laughed so hard that he almost flipped over in his chair, then he dried a tiny tear and sighed in astonishment, "what a great people we are."

XV

After his dinner with Rosa, Alfredo spent the weekend doing nothing, his favorite activity, and meditating. On Saturday morning he went to the Griddle for breakfast. The Griddle is one of those greasy spoons from a bygone America where waitresses hitting their seventies, chomping on chewing gum, continuously walk around with a glass pot full of fresh coffee and ask you *some more coffee, hon?* whether you're in your twenties or you're a hundred, whether they're talking to a child or a pimp. They ask *are your eggs good, hon?* in their accents from the Deep South, wearing so much red lipstick that you always wonder what they were like when they were young, these decent old women in pink aprons, what dreams they had back in Mississippi.

In any case, the eggs were always good, God forbid they weren't, and Alfredo was reading the Sun Sentinel feeling like he was in a Robert Altman movie, but that morning he was thinking about Rosa. An unexpected sadness came over him, engulfed him. Not so much her story, but one image – the eyes of that child, defenseless, innocent. They way he was looking into the camera, like a tiny, flustered animal. He thought about his mother who went to visit him every day, about his father who never wanted to see him. He felt a mixture of tenderness and bitterness that gave him a lump in his throat. He left money for the check and a sizable tip, then went on his way.

Next to the Griddle is a wonderful used book store, Bookwise, a kind of cavernous space guarded by two fat cats who appear and disappear behind piles of dusty books, like mysterious Indian deities. Mrs. Arlette owns the cats and the store. Very old and very tall, quiet and reserved, she also often vanishes, perhaps to adjust the moonshine stills in some subterranean laboratory whose entrance is hidden behind the bookshelves, there's no other explanation. If you want to buy a book you have to wait until she returns from finishing her magic or slip away discretely with the book. That morning Alfredo bought a volume of poetry by Keats, an Oxford University Press 1912 edition, with an introduction and comments by Buxton Forman, and he spent the rest of his Sunday stretched out on the boiling hot sand, a few feet from the crystal-clear water, under an azure sky imbued with light, while the afternoon absorbed even the smallest ray of sunlight as it passed ever so slowly over the gently lapping ocean and the squawking seagulls. He was reading Keats and drinking beer, squinting until his eyes were almost closed, letting his eyelashes veil his view of the world, transforming it into an exquisitely blurred mass of azures, blues and British verse. And then his thoughts turned to Rosa and her child. And he thought about God. He had never been an atheist, but God's negligence in this case seemed appalling to him. And yet, it was appealing to that same God that Rosa had endured, she had accepted her destiny and was speaking about it to Alfredo in a steady voice while sipping her coffee. The biggest mystery of all is the human being.

XVI

The following day the sky was gray and the threat of rain loomed in the air. Rosa and Alfredo sat breathing in the humid morning air and slowly drinking their coffees, smoking their cigarettes.

"The fact that you got married so young does it hinge on what happened in Calabria?"

"What's up with you Fred, you writing a book?" She answered smiling, with her cigarette dangling between her teeth.

Alfredo jokingly pointed his finger near her face, "my dear Rosa, you started it!"

She grabbed his finger with a sudden, brusque gesture, then held it gently, regained her composure, and added softly, "don't point your finger at me, Fred…"

Alfredo was annoyed, "Rosa, I was joking."

"Sorry, Fred. It's just that a pointed finger is how the whole thing started. That's the first image."

"The first image?"

"Yes, I misled you… that is, I should have told you right off the bat: a pointed finger. And then: seven laughing children. And then: a poor house, extremely poor. And then: my parents. And then: a little girl who's no longer laughing. But the pointed finger comes before the rest. I pieced together the other images around the pointed finger. That pointed finger has persecuted me, still persecutes me, at night I see that finger and I feel my chest caving in, I feel my legs giving out, I feel that finger piercing my heart and I feel the deepest, darkest desperation, the most intense sadness."

"Is that what you felt when the finger was pointed at you?"

"Maybe. It's what I began to feel night after night, image after image. When I hadn't yet assembled all the details and I was young, but not so young, and day after day I grew older and I put the pieces together like you're doing. You understand?"

"I think so."

"I no longer know what I felt then, at that precise instant, terror maybe, but I know what I felt after, I know what I feel now when I see that finger again and I know what it means. But not for me, you know, not for my suffering… but for that little girl… I was so young, so young… I was three years old, Holy Christ, how can you do such a thing to a three year old child?"

Alfredo didn't know what to say. Bizarre looking white birds with long orange-colored beaks, similar to miniature cranes, were strolling near them. Two squirrels were playing and images of pointed fingers flashed through Alfred's mind, *The Last Judgement*, obviously, and Plato in *The School of Athens*, Manet's *The Conservatory*, a *Bacchus* by da Vinci, Dalì's *Metamorphosis* and finally the poster of Uncle Sam snarling, I WANT YOU! The fact is that, because he was always looking at paintings, Alfredo is unable to meet anyone or to do anything without his mind referencing this or that picture, like the pedantic bibliography of a boring scholarly paper, almost wanting to establish that someone and that something are real and legitimate or that instead his whole life is nothing but an imitation.

But now it was time to go back to the cafeteria. Alfredo understood, but kept quiet. He thought about Uncle Jeffrey and Aunt Lisa, "so, basically your parents sent you to America, to live with your Aunt Lisa, your mother's or your father's sister?"

"My mother was an only child and my father only had brothers."

"Okay, then Uncle Jeffrey must be your father's brother, it's six of one and half a dozen of the other."

"Excuse me but does Jeffrey seem like a Calabrian name to you?"

"Dammit, that's right. But who is Jeffrey then?"

"My mother's sister's husband." She laughed, like she had just cracked the joke of the century.

"Rosa, you mean you have two mothers?"

"I *had* two mothers. They're both dead."

"I'm sorry."

"So am I, all in all."

XVII

Alfredo thought about it all afternoon. That night he called her, "Rosa…did you also have a second father?"

"Yes."

"Father and mother number two… were they also in the room?"

"Yes, Fred, you got it…"

"Which one of the four pointed the finger at you?"

"My American mother."

"Your biological Italian parents gave you up for adoption to your adoptive American parents?"

"No Fred. They sold me. The way I sell hamburgers now."

XVIII

1955. Calabria, the southernmost part of Italy. In a powerful voice, a man calls his seven children. Here they are, some are coming in from playing outside and some from the only bedroom. Suddenly they notice two strangers, a man and a woman, and they are spellbound. They are beautifully dressed, but very serious, not smiling at all. The seven children hear the imperious voice of their father ordering them to line up. Their mother is whimpering on a chair with her elbows on the table, her body limp, her head in her hands. Why is she crying? The children are smiling and laughing. They have never seen anyone as elegant as these two people, but they sense that something is going to happen, they feel a jolt of nervous tension go right through them straight to their hearts. The oldest is fourteen years old, a long-limbed boy with an olive-colored complexion, and he's anxious; the second girl, almost twelve, is unruly, filthy hair with eyes like bottomless wells; the third girl, eleven years old, is scratching her head and sniffling; the fourth child, maybe nine years old, is a little girl with the chubby face of a piglet and all of a sudden she starts crying; the fifth one, seven years old, is looking at her wondering why her sister is crying, because their mother is crying; the sixth girl is very beautiful, has a healthy glow, ruddy cheeks, and is out of breath, smiling joyfully – still caught up in the game she was playing, hardly bothered by the interruption – she's smiling but something has rattled her, the beauty of those clothes, that woman whose face is partially hidden by a small veil, she feels a slight tremor in her chest, stares at her crying mother, turns toward her year and a half old little brother, next to her, who is suddenly shrieking. The lady in the veiled hat whispers something into the ear of the gentleman, who nods and whispers something into her father's ear; her mother, seated at the table with her head in her hands, suddenly lifts her head up, her tear-soaked eyes are now wide-open, and she looks directly at the lady, who, from behind her veil, meets that sorrowful gaze for a moment, quickly turns her head toward the children, raises her arm and points her finger at the sixth child, still intent on consoling her little brother. The little girl hears a deafening silence, then the impulsive muffled howl of her mother, and tilts her tiny head slowly toward the lady, smiling, but sees the finger pointed at her, this large finger, steady, unwavering, aiming at her like a pistol ready to shoot; she stops smiling, her lips start quivering, a sense of impending doom permeates her body, like something has grabbed her heart, taking her breath away, making her legs tremble. She is stunned, her father goes into the bedroom and comes back with her rag doll, shoves it into her hand, then pushes her toward the strangers (she feels her father's forceful hand on her back). Her brothers are quiet, even the smallest one, her mother is hiding her face in her hands and is sobbing (that sobbing is like a gavel) – but what is going to happen? Now the lady takes her hand, she doesn't move, but she again feels the pressure of her father's hand behind her, she places her hand in the lady's, goes outside with the strangers and her father. Suddenly she hears the door slam shut behind her, she turns around, her father is no longer there and a cry of terror rises from her legs, from the pit of her stomach, from her heart and it then transforms into a horrifying scream, like a giant roar, becoming even more heartrending when the gentleman grabs her by the waist, drags her away and places her in the back seat of a large car. He sits beside her, while the lady with the veiled hat gets in on the other side. "Go, go!" The gentleman yells at the driver, now the little girl is also yelling – then the lady shows her a large, creamy dessert sprinkled with candied fruit, gives it to her and she immediately quiets down, astonished, incredulous, that this dessert is real and that it's for her, just for her. She touches it, puts it in her mouth, it's fantastic, she devours it and is distracted.

The couple and the small child left for America the same evening.

XIX

Rosa grew up on Long Island. The two Americans who bought her had never been happy: is it ever possible to be happy on Long Island? They were rich enough – the American guy owned a chain of hardware stores – but they were not happy. In an attempt to look for the happiness which they had never found, they decided to travel. They ended up in Italy, which they crisscrossed from the big cities to the South where, one evening, the American got plastered in a low class dive in a small coastal town, after the umpteenth fight with his wife, and met an old fisherman as desperate as he was. In that common language, perhaps prodigiously born from the alcohol, they both let off steam, the American tormented because he and his wife were unable to have children and the Calabrian guy troubled by too many mouths to feed. His wife just kept cranking out kids, the hunger so painful that they resorted to cooking rats, and then one offered to buy a child from the other: maybe at the outset it was a joke prompted by the wine, but then the idea gained traction and cohesiveness. With the help of the innkeeper, who had been a prisoner of war in the United States and spoke very good English, they began shooting the breeze, negotiated the price, discussed the bureaucratic red tape and the possibility of finding an accommodating notary so that the following day, after speaking to their respective wives, the transaction concluded with a pointed finger.

XX

Of course, this was the story based on Rosa's reminiscences. It was a story full of gaps, contradictions and ambiguity fueled by subsequent nightmares, inventions and betrayals of a three-year-old child's memory, by what Rosa discovered later on, always filtered through other people's stories and points of view. Only when she was twenty years old, after years of flashbacks creeping to the surface and then plunging into an abyss of images, and after years when unknown words, whose meanings baffled her, became mixed in with her English vocabulary, did Rosa manage to put together a sufficient number of the pieces to the puzzle to get a good grip on her story. The American gentleman had been dead for a while. Rosa barely even remembered him: he was cold, stand-offish and terribly unhappy, had neglected his business until he slowly went broke, divorced his wife when Rosa was seven years old, moved out west, risked everything he had left playing blackjack and died there, another cheap drunk.

Rosa's American mother started drinking as well, vacillating between moments of tenderness and fits of uncontrolled rage, until one day she loaded up the back seat of the car with suitcases and, with Rosa in the front, they left for a very long trip. Together they traveled down the East Coast in her mother's old black Buick, experienced an incredibly beautiful scenic panorama that filled Rosa's eyes with a previously unknown happiness, and when she saw the ocean it provoked an inexplicable nostalgia. Her mother, in black sunglasses with a green scarf wrapped around her head, drove and drove, smoking, knocking back whiskey from a small round bottle, taking the curves too fast. Rosa didn't dare interrupt the extended silences, letting herself revel in the turquoise light of a Pennsylvania afternoon, the stark whiteness of the large colonial houses in Virginia and the dark forests of North Carolina. Her mother would occasionally break her silence by bursting into sudden laughter, she started talking about her husband, as if she were resuming an interrupted conversation, telling Rosa how they had met, how they had fallen in love, then quickly retreated into absolute silence once again. But it really didn't matter all that much to Rosa, her only question was where they were headed (she was suddenly panic-stricken that her mother wanted to abandon her on the side of the road or in the bushes somewhere) so she felt reassured when her mother told her that they were going to visit her sister Lisa, her brother-in-law Jeffrey and their son Jonathan – your little cousin, "just think, Rosette!"

Rosa didn't really like it when her mother called her Rosette, but she also knew that her mother sometimes called her Rosette instead of Rosa because her mother liked anything French and Rosa didn't dare contradict her. Besides, the only thing that interested Rosa was that trip which she was thoroughly enjoying: she liked the red gas stations where they stopped to refuel, the dusty roads that went on forever, that sky which changed colors from morning till night, from state to state, often from gray to the coolest shade of blue to pale pink to deep blue, she was crazy about the diners they stopped at, so her mother could fill up on coffee while she could pig out on fried chicken a go-go.

XXI

"It took us three days, Fred but I still remember that trip."

"And how long did you stay with Lisa and Jeffrey?" Asked Alfredo.

"A month, maybe longer. Then we went back up north. I remember that I was a mess, but Uncle Jeffrey and Aunt Lisa were unbelievable, even my mother seemed less stressed out, she smiled more, and Jonathan was great too, like the brother I never had, rather, that I didn't know I had…" Rosa smiled bringing the coffee to her lips.

"Was it Aunt Lisa and Uncle Jeffrey who told you the truth?"

"Hold on, don't rush me… it took *me* twenty years to learn the truth. We returned to Long Island. But things went straight to hell. Suddenly I no longer went to school, my mother had taken me out. She was only getting worse. She was drinking and was a nervous wreck, and I became her servant. Even in the middle of the night, 'Rosette, water! Rosette, a sandwich!' I ran to the kitchen, made her a cucumber sandwich, the only thing she would eat, and refilled her glass with cold water, and then I would invariably find her asleep, on her unmade bed, between the dirty sheets and pillows. At the end of the summer, my mother told me 'tomorrow we're going back to Aunt Lisa's.' I couldn't believe it! What happiness, Fred, such utter joy!"

"They're good people then, Lisa, Jeffrey and Jonathan?"

"The best, Fred. That's the most beautiful part of this story. They are my family."

XXII

"That time we stayed there several months, I couldn't say how long for sure. And yet, my mother always seemed calmer, but I remember that she also seemed older, more worn out. That was the only thing that made me sad. I started school again here in Florida, Jonathan and I used to take a yellow school bus every morning, we had lunch together, we played on the beach every day and I stopped having nightmares. It was a fairy tale, but the one black cloud was my mother. So one night when she took me aside and told me, 'I'm going home tomorrow, I have to be there to take care of some business' – my blood froze! But then she asked me, 'Are you okay staying here with Aunt Lisa, Uncle Jeffrey and Jonathan?' I hated to see her so despondent, so resigned, but what a relief, Fred, what a relief!"

"I believe it. And you never went back to Long Island?"

The look on Rosa's face was lost somewhere, wandering among the light blues of the sky. "Hold your horses. My mother used to write and come down two or three times a year. Each time she brought bags of stuff, mine and hers: filthy, tattered clothes, and toys I didn't play with anymore, I don't know why she didn't just throw it all away, instead she brought it all with her little by little. She no longer had the nervous ticks nor did she ask me to make her sandwiches, during the day or at night: that bothered me a little bit. She was so thin, and so old, and seemed so lost, she used to look out the window and babble on, talking about her husband, my father, and she would look at me with those runny eyes and tell me desultory details about a trip to Italy, and I hadn't even the slightest idea where that was."

"Good God!"

"And then, with each passing day, re-energized, she started smiling again, plaintively, and stopped that inane rambling and decided that it was time to leave again, even though her sister tried to convince her to stay – but she left anyway."

"But how did she support herself?"

"I don't know and I don't want to know. But it certainly must not have been enough, because then she came back, until one day she returned for the last time. I was almost seventeen years old. I had become a beautiful young woman, Fred, my breasts had developed and I had a nice figure. And I remember that I was unloading bags full of junk from the Buick, and there I was, throwing things out without even looking at them, as usual, until I saw something funny that was poking out, a small bundle, an enigma that caught my attention: I pulled it out. It was a rag doll."

XXIII

"You're Italian" her mother told her on her deathbed, between rambling, fragmented stories and muffled cries. She left this world within a week, but that wasn't the most upsetting thing: Rosa watched over her day and night, torn between the suffering of that shattered woman and the turmoil the rag doll had provoked in her. Visions were piling up in her mind, arbitrarily, between running to the sink to dampen a facecloth to place on her mother's feverish forehead and unintentionally nodding off while she was slowly swaying in the rocking chair next to her mother's bed – images of a stone house, of seven children lined up, of a pointed finger. Her mother took her hand, in those moments when she was lucid, telling her, "if you only knew how beautiful the place you come from is!" Rosa rolled her eyes, "from where, from where, ma? Ma?" The woman became very sad, and started crying softly, "but such misery, such misery," she said, "you were so lucky, my daughter" and she laughed, she laughed nervously, then she fell asleep. Rosa turned toward her aunt and uncle who looked directly at one other and confessed that they didn't know much, they knew nothing: Aunt Lisa was already living in Florida when, twelve to thirteen years earlier, her sister had written telling her she was pregnant. During the pregnancy she continued to write, detailing the nausea and the dizziness, and she especially complained about her husband. She described the birth, wrote that they had named the baby Rosa, that she had blue eyes and golden curls, *she looks exactly like me, fortunately nothing like Wilfred.* But then, eight years after those letters Aunt Lisa finally saw her niece, met her sister again, and realized there was something fishy going on since Rosa didn't look anything like her mother and she was at least four to five years older than she supposedly should have been.

"Did she corner her sister, confront her?" Asked Alfredo.

"Of course not. It was too embarrassing. Besides, my mother didn't conceal my age: she simply said I was the age I was, she had completely forgotten about those letters and my aunt never mentioned them, it was just too embarrassing. Now remember, we're in America and don't ever forget that. Here, distance has a tendency to cause everything to unravel, there's always the risk of becoming estranged. Even me, my children.... I haven't seen Tommasina in five years. If I don't call her, who hears from her?"

"So Aunt Lisa acted as if nothing was wrong."

"Or else she convinced herself that we were blood relatives, who knows. But she went to Long Island with me after the funeral and helped me empty drawers and boxes of documents, the only things that my mother had not brought down to Florida with her. Then I found everything, I found a piece of paper with the signatures of my two fathers and that asshole notary, and I found out my last name."

XXIV

"I had no money, because even the house in Long Island went into foreclosure. The only thing I had left was an armoire with clothes that didn't fit me anymore – and a rag doll. I had to go to Italy. Aunt Lisa and Uncle Jeffrey didn't have enough money for two tickets, but they managed to scrape together the money for one ticket. I was almost eighteen years old, it was in '68, I landed in Rome at the height of summer and after two trains I finally reached my little village in Calabria."

"What a tremendously emotional..."

"No, I was too exhausted. It was scorching hot, it was August. I walked five miles from the station, then I accepted a ride from someone whose cart was being pulled by a donkey. It was the most desolate place I've ever seen, there were only rocks, rocks and stones, stones and rocks. I started asking anyone I came across questions: an old woman who was busy darning socks in front of a crumbling hovel, a vagabond, even two children who were playing with a dead snake. But no one understood a fucking word of English or they pretended not to. I looked around and didn't recognize anything. At one point I thought I'd made a big mistake. I found a tavern, asked for something to eat, I was ravenous, and I needed a bed, 'io mangiare, io bere,' I said. The innkeeper had a ruddy face, a wisp of blond hair fell on his forehead, he stared at me and for a moment I was scared. There wasn't a soul in the place. The innkeeper put out some goat cheese, a very long salami, a hunk of bread and a bowl of black olives. Without saying a word he brought me to a table and starting slicing the salami and cheese with a hunting knife that sent shivers down my spine. I was terrified. Then he went behind the counter, took out a pitcher of red wine, came over and sat next to me, 'it's nice to meet you', he said, in perfect English."

XXV

"The innkeeper that was there when your two fathers met!!!" Exclaimed an astounded Alfredo.

"Yes, him. And he immediately recognized me. 'You are Rosa,' he said. Initially he seemed sure of himself. But then, as he was speaking, there was an infinite sadness in his eyes and he was unable to look directly into mine: you know, I think that he was ashamed..."

"Of course. It was his fault too."

"Huh! He said 'that these two people,' my two fathers, as you put it, 'started talking, drinking, laughing, and then they started crying... on a night as black as coal,' he continued 'even though it was summer... there was no one in the tavern... times were tough then'..."

This is how it happened: "This American had shown up, strange and taciturn, the countenance of a broken man, dressed like a very rich man, and he asked the innkeeper for a room for himself and his wife. It was an event, and the news spread like wildfire among the villagers. The innkeeper didn't have to think twice about making some extra pocket change and prepared his own room for the Americans while he went to sleep in the bathtub. In the ensuing days, the American's wife, hardly ever seen by anyone, invariably shut herself up in the room, while the man, on the other hand, came down, ate, drank quite a bit and spent a fair amount of money. He seemed happy to have finally found someone who spoke English and passed entire evenings conversing with the innkeeper, especially about the war. Every night the men of the village would gather around a small table, near the American and the innkeeper, where they sat fascinated, listening in silence, to their incomprehensible conversations, and the American would buy everyone drinks. Finally, one 'cursed evening', as the innkeeper characterized it, when everyone else had gone home to sleep, my Italian father approached the table and joined the two of them. He and my future American father began to confide in each other and at a certain point they began tossing around an idea, a plan that mesmerized them, while the innkeeper kept translating, translating everything..."

I thought they were joking, said the innkeeper, trying to justify his involvement to Rosa, unable to look her in the eyes, his voice and his hands trembling, continuing to slice the salami – Rosa was no longer eating, she just stared at him, petrified – and the innkeeper said that all three of them were drunk, really shit-faced, and that they heard the dogs howling in the surrounding hills and the thundering roar of the ocean. He said that at a certain point he stopped translating because he stopped laughing and he stopped laughing because they had stopped laughing and they became serious, and he no longer liked the tone of their voices or the looks on their faces, but it was so late, so very late, soon it would be daybreak, soon it would all be nothing more than a bad dream – but the following day there was no longer any trace of little Rosa in the village.

XXVI

Thanks to the innkeeper and his valuable assistance, Rosa managed to get a telephone number and called her family in Trieste. A woman answered. Her mother? Rosa's heart was stuck in her throat. But the voice was too young. Her sister? "Sono Rosa…" she murmured in Italian. A terrifying silence followed. "Cosa?" And Rosa heard an echo of bewilderment and incredulity in that voice, and she repeated, "sono Rosa…." Then a scream: "Rosa!!!…. Rosa!!!" A sudden chaotic screaming erupted from beyond the phone, and Rosa felt a smile emerging on her face, a rush of joy, she felt imbued with good feelings: they were happy to hear her, her presence brought them happiness. For a few seconds she only heard the increasing number of voices screaming "Rosa!!! Rosa!!!" Then finally: "sorella mia!!! Sei davvero tu?! Dove sei?! Come stai?!" But at this point Rosa didn't understand much of anything, between the emotion that was gripping her throat and that quaking voice which overwhelmed her with sounds she didn't understand. Unable to utter a single word, she looked at the innkeeper, who understood and took the receiver: when they had all calmed down on the other end of the line, he explained everything. The next day he accompanied her to the train station, helped her carry her suitcases and buy a ticket, hugged her, and Rosa left for Rome and from Rome she went on to Trieste.

"What a trip! What a trip, Fred… every emotion in the world was percolating in me…"

Alfredo was watching her, stunned, by now his coffee was cold, he was drawn in by her facial features while she was telling him her incredible story, he saw the little blonde curls pocking out of her work cap, the dark incandescence in her eyes, and what he now saw was the eighteen-year-old Rosa, curled up in an old compartment of a small antiquated train from the '60s, devouring the bread and the salami from the straw basket that the innkeeper had prepared, smelling the old leather seats, observing Italy in black and white racing by outside her little window, her heart quivering from the most intense emotions. Alfredo could not even begin to imagine how she felt and it seemed impossible to him that the human heart could process all these emotions at the same time, the joy of finding your family again, the joy she now felt so profoundly because she had heard them, she had heard them screaming ecstatically, had heard them calling her 'my sister', and she searched her fragmented memory, she concentrated on finding an image, she even tried sleeping to capture in her dreams those faces that had sometimes crossed her mind in a frenzy – but then one question tormented her: why hadn't they looked for her? And then her mother, *her mother*, her mother who had given her to another woman, the rage, the fear, Alfredo wondered what she had felt, he would have liked to ask her about it but maybe not even she knew anymore, he saw her put out her cigarette in what was left of her coffee, get up from the little table, telling him that it was time to go back to work, and he also got up, his cigarette still burning between his fingers, the sky was blue and they walked toward the cafeteria and the young Rosa on the tiny train was getting closer to Trieste, dreaming, trembling, her insides roaring.

At the station in Trieste she got off the train not even feeling the exhaustion of the trip or the weight of her suitcases, her hands were sweating, her temples were pounding frenetically, she let herself be enveloped by the chaos of the people who were hurrying to exit the station, by the whistling and the screeching of the trains, by the smells of sweat and scrap iron, and she peeked out the small windows but her view was blurred and finally she was outside: like a magnet she didn't even need to look in the middle of the crowd: she saw four girls and a boy younger than she. Their eyes and their mouths were wide open, and in a bizarre twist of fate they were lined up, one next to the other, the youngest last, and Rosa's eyes and mouth were wide open as well and they remained there, for the longest moment, like they were enclosed in a giant soap bubble, and then Rosa took a few steps and she saw tears in those wide-open eyes and felt tears in her own and, as if under some magic spell, all six of them hugged each other in a unique embrace filled with sobbing, kisses, subdued tears, uninterrupted, tears that said it all, and no one said a word.

XXVII

"Am I wrong or was your older brother missing?" Asked Alfredo.

"Giuseppe. Giuseppe's an asshole. He lives in Como, with his wife and kids. He was already married, at that time, and wasn't really interested at all in the rest of his family, least of all me. I think I met him for the first time a year later, and he treated me like a perfect stranger. What a selfish dick! According to my sisters, he's a carbon copy of my father. And the only one who could have looked for me…"

"What about your older sisters…" ventured Alfredo, immediately biting his tongue for being so blunt. But Rosa defended them right away.

"No, I understand them. Women's lives were terrible back then. It was disgraceful. Above all they had to think of feeding themselves and defending themselves against that father and that brother. They needed to get away from them as soon as possible, they had no time to think about me. And how could they? Who knew where I was? The only thing they knew was that I was certainly better off than they were, this was what my mother had told them, even if they couldn't talk about me at home. I was as good as dead."

"It must have been amazing, for them, to find you again..." said Alfredo trying to make up for his insensitivity.

"Oh, they really love me, Fred! We're inseparable. We talk to each other every week. You know, I speak to my sisters and my brother Francesco and my nieces and nephews more than I do to my own children. It's because we're Italian, my children are American, there's not much I can do about it. Not that my kids don't love me, for God's sake, they would die for me, but they don't feel compelled to call, to chit chat, like we Italians do, understand? You for example, how often do you speak to your mother?"

Alfredo was embarrassed to tell the truth (almost every day, between phone calls and emails) and was deliberately vague, "often. But I have a lot of free time."

"Of course. My kids work their asses off, uh for as much as they work, and they have mortgages and cars to pay for... life isn't easy."

XXVIII

I met Alfredo Crepuscolo a few months after he came to Boca, after he had been accepted into the Master's Program and hired as an assistant professor to teach introductory Art History courses at Florida Atlantic University. Life in Boca was much more expensive than in Indiana, at least as much as living in a medium-sized or large Italian city: compared to Italy there were some things that cost more and other things that cost less, so Alfredo became very sensible in his choices, he gave up wine, Parmigiano cheese and to a large extent fruits and vegetables, enthusiastically embracing a diet of pasta, bread and sausages. He gained a lot of weight and his blood tests showed excessively high triglycerides, so he decided he had to make more money and eat better. The student visa, that the university had procured for Alfredo, did not permit him to work off campus: luckily, he had arrived in America at the right time, when Italy epitomized everything that Americans longed for, everything they wanted to be. Art, beauty, the love for family and food, the Mafia, everything that was considered quintessentially Italian, was irresistible to Americans. Italians, they said (and everyone said it, without exception) *know how to live*, and this was an indisputable supposition, a truth that didn't need any proof. Italy was all the rage and everyone wanted to speak Italian, travel to Italy, live in Italy. The students whose parents didn't know a word of Italian, because their Italian fathers had refused to teach them, wanted to learn Italian so they could speak to their grandparents. It was the beginning of a new century and those were dark times for America. At least on campus, where Alfredo was living, you could hear young and old alike putting down their own country, going on anti-American tirades for waging a futile war, ashamed of being Americans and wanting to run away to Italy. For various Italian intellectuals in the '40s America appeared as a mirage of freedom in contrast to the harsh chains of fascism, and so Italy, sixty years later, seemed like the cradle of civilization to Americans, a place where you could live a truly meaningful life.

Alfredo didn't comment on any of this, and anyway he had his triglycerides to worry about. So one morning he showed up at my office in the Department of Languages and Linguistics, he introduced himself, firmly shook my hand and he asked me if I could give out his phone number to those Italian students who were looking for a private tutor. Of course, I answered, and then I advised him to check out the Department of Continuing Education, because they were always looking for qualified instructors. The Department of Continuing Ed, which offers evening courses to people who do not need a degree but just want to learn, offered Alfredo the chance to teach a weekly two-hour Italian class, ten sessions for seven hundred dollars. His students were, for the most part, over sixty years old, retired, and always cheerful: they spent the two hours of the lesson discussing recipes and wines, and they had a great time. There was Leonard, a guy with a potbelly who was always smiling and frantically taking notes with a miniscule pen, his wife Lois, who never managed to correctly trill her r's and usually ended up giggling along with the rest of the class, Annabella, who had a daughter in Bologna, and Rita, a seventy-year old Irish woman who had raised five children on her own, witnessed the birth of close to twenty grandchildren, watched them all grow up and now spent every summer in Florence staying at a convent, and then there were Ruth, Gonzalo, Carol and a few others, each one having his or her own reasons, who were as thrilled as school kids when they could say "Posso avere un caffè per favore?"

On the evening of the last lesson each student brought homemade food, some brought spinach dip, others brought cold pasta salad and brownies. Elizabeth, the oldest of the group, made an enormous chocolate cake with whipped cream and lightly toasted slivered almonds, and since more than half the cake was left over everyone insisted that the professor take it home: he snacked on it for three weeks.

Alfredo started putting up flyers around town, at the university, in a few Italian American restaurants, in Sonny's gelato shop – the one with the life-sized wax figure of Dean Martin in the window – offering private Italian lessons for $30.00 an hour. The response was overwhelming. There was the student who needed to recoup a solid standing in his Italian class (he asked the student for $20.00), there was the old opera conductor who was ashamed because he didn't know the language used in *La Traviata* well enough, and there were the millionaire art collectors who had bought small country houses in Umbria because they wanted to spend six months a year in Italy (he asked them for $40.00).

He managed to earn enough from tutoring which allowed him to move from the campus dormitory when he had lived up until then: besides, in the beginning it had been fun, the parties, the girls and the kegs of beer, but the thrill of living the fast-paced life of an American student quickly soured. He shared a room with Strauss, a very tall and very disorganized Austrian guy who was studying music, snored like a trombone, and left sheet music, dirty bicycle tires and boxes of Mexican food, the only thing he ate, scattered all over the room. He was not unlikable, though he was pretty homely, he had buck teeth, was cross-eyed, wore thick glasses and his hair looked like a mop had been grafted onto his head: Alfredo asked him about Vienna, which he had never seen, and about Prater Stadium. But Strauss didn't understand anything about soccer and Alfredo didn't understand anything about Mozart, so the conversations languished and were limited to smiling at each other in a show of solidarity. They shared a disgusting bathroom on the floor below with three other guys and, with all the other students on their floor, a putrid kitchen, always filthy with sauce stains, that had a foul smell from the discarded cans. Maybe ten years earlier all this would have seemed adventurous and less skeevy than it now seemed, but now he was over thirty-years old and over the need to stay up until dawn drinking beer until he got sick – in case he ever did – and he learned to more diligently cultivate his enjoyment of solitude. When he found a very small apartment, five minutes from the university by bike for $500 a month, it seemed like he had found Paradise.

XXIX

It was similar to Rosa's apartment – which he had yet to visit: there was a miniscule kitchen separated from the living room by a waist-high wall, and on the other side was a beautiful light-colored wood table with four straw-bottomed chairs, painted blue; on the other side near the large sliding glass doors which opened onto the balcony, an old Bahamas style couch, a coffee table and a decent TV with cable. A hallway led to a small bathroom on one side and, on the other, was the bedroom, furnished with a bed, even too large for him, and a small desk above which a couple of boards had been nailed to the wall, serving as makeshift bookshelves. The morning sunlight filtered through the window, lit up the spines of his art history book collection, a framed reproduction of a Toulouse-Lautrec painting and his cherished notebook, with the well-worn cover, that he used as a diary and left open. The intoxicating thrill of freedom and independence lasted for quite some time and Alfredo couldn't wait to come home at night to bone up on his reading or enjoy a brandy while watching a movie. Then, sometimes, boredom reared its ugly head, like a bitter herb, exposing the dark side of his solitude – so he frequently organized small parties for his friends, would go to dinner with Professor Sciagarone and his wife, or to the movies with me. He asked a few girls out and, for lack of something better to do, he even saw Strauss – in this way he could once again appreciate the pure pleasure of being alone.

XXX

One Saturday Rosa invited Alfredo to dinner. He arrived early, so they decided to take a stroll by the ocean. To get there, you had to walk across a wooden footbridge, since the tropical vegetation separated the street from the beach. Meeting her Italian mother, as Rosa called her, was dramatic. Alfredo tried to get her to go into more detail as she told her story, but for the first time he saw her stumble over her words, get confused, her face looked drawn and she nervously exhaled smoke, like a skittish horse. She never got upset, at least not visibly, when she spoke of her dead three year old little son, nor when she spoke about her husband's physical abuse or her American mother or how she had found her siblings. She managed to keep her emotions in check, organized her thoughts, and the words flowed out precisely and clearly. But meeting her mother, her true biological mother, that face which haunted her dreams, the echo of her crying as she watched her three year old being taken from her, the helplessness of not being able to distance herself from her overbearing husband's resolve – what Rosa had lived through and didn't remember but now imagined and pieced together inside herself – all of this still traumatized her.

XXXI

They were walking by the water's edge around five o'clock. There was a peacefulness that enveloped everything, not a breath of wind, no one walking except the two of them, the temperature was mild, the boundless sky, gray and blue, unleashed long clouds unraveling in shades of amber, not even the seagulls were squawking. The beach was a strip of deserted sand, strewn with seaweed and shells, and it went on forever, between the indigenous vegetation and the ocean. Even the ocean was extremely calm, as unflappable as an English gentleman, a mirror of crystalline water that faded into hues of light blue and cobalt blue, and offshore you could see small silver fish jumping to the surface: it was as if the elements of nature were intent on listening to Rosa's story, in order to draw out of her the particulars of that formidable encounter with her Italian mother.

"You know, the sensation I most remember... was that until that moment I felt like a grown-up... I always felt like a grown-up: compared to my American mother, compared to my cousin Jonathan, even compared to my Aunt Lisa and my Uncle Jeffrey... and even compared to my brothers and sisters at the train station: I was practically the youngest, but I felt older. What I mean is, *the oldest*. The others were all children, not me. I... I was the one who took care of them, who had to protect them, do you understand, Fred?"

"Of course I do."

"But the time was approaching to meet this woman. I was twisted like a pretzel in the front seat of my sister Carmela's Fiat 600 because my brother Francesco was in the back holding my sister Maria in his lap, and my sisters Flora and Lucia were holding the suitcases in their arms, I still really don't know how we managed to get six people plus the two suitcases into a 600... uh, what was I saying?"

"That you always felt old."

"Oh right. But the time to meet my mother was quickly getting closer, I was surrounded by my brothers and sisters who were talking and talking and talking and I didn't understand a damned thing but I was happy and I could feel my chest shaking violently from the tremendous excitement, because I was happy but I was also sad because I didn't understand what my siblings were saying and it wasn't right, it just wasn't right, and I was overcome with a hidden, deep-seated rage and then I knew, I knew that I was about to meet my mother, more so because the only word I understood was *mamma*... So, we slowly went on our way, parked, got out of the car, went up the stairs and... it was like regressing to my childhood with each step... I felt like a little girl, younger with each step... there we were... and when the door opened..."

A large pelican dove into the water, determined to grab a fish and Rosa stopped, because the memory became intolerable. I remained silent, but I saw, I saw one of her sisters open the door and the young Rosa plow through the door, trembling, but now my imagination had also transformed her into a little girl again, the same little girl with the most beautiful ruddy cheeks that I had pictured when she was lined up with the other six, in a room in an old house in Calabria, the same little girl I had seen screaming, defenseless and terrified, screaming at her mother, a young woman who was crying with her head in her hands, left alone on a chair in front of a table, and now I saw this child again catapulted into the center of another room, so tiny, but no longer defenseless and terrified, I have to say, facing that same woman, her mother, and her mother is still there, limp on a chair in front of a table, with her head in her hands, and she's crying.

"There was a scream... my mother screamed, she got up... she hugged me tightly, almost smothering me... I don't know where she got the strength from, because she was so thin... she was screaming, and everyone was screaming and bawling ... a real mess... only I was no longer crying."

XXXII

As usual Rosa cooked enough for an army. Little calzone stuffed with garlic and cheese, macaroni *all'arrabbiata,* fiery hot from the red pepper flakes, veal *al marsala,* baked potatoes with sour cream, an enormous salad with shrimp, pineapple, celery and ginger, the bottle of Chilean wine that Alfredo had brought, Sicilian style cannolis glazed with chocolate, coffee and Wild Turkey. You couldn't say no to her, Alfredo had barely finished eating what was on his plate and Rosa refilled it, "eat, you're much too thin," she said, and he ate, because no one ever had to beg him to eat, and he felt the wine dissolving in his veins and a vague nostalgia for his home, for the affectionate attention of his mom, for the conversations with his brother, for his father's lasagna and the soccer games they enjoyed watching on TV together, for the vacations by the beach when they were young. Alfredo asked her, "what was your mother like?"

"Which one?"

"The Italian one."

"She was old. Sickly. And we spoke two different languages, just like I did with my brothers and sisters. But I'm smart and I learn things. Even with my kids at Burger King, Fred, do you think I speak English? Spanish, Fred. Spanish. If I speak English they don't understand me and it would take a half hour to make them do things the way they should be done. And besides, this way they respect me more, they love me more, because I come down to their level. And you know where I learned Spanish? With them, listening to them talk, and with a grammar book at home. Can you believe it?"

Her eyes gleamed with pride and for a moment she forgot about her mother. I raised my glass to toast her, "here's to you, Rosa!"

XXXIII

"I started studying Italian as much as I could, because I needed to communicate. I also started working, thanks to my sister Carmela, cleaning offices with her. My siblings and I began talking, day after day, week after week. Carmela had very few memories of that day when they took me away, because the shit would have hit the fan if anyone talked about it at home. Our father, or as you prefer to call him that animal, took off his belt if my name was mentioned. So everyone tried to erase any memory of me, but some things don't go away and my older siblings used to talk about me among themselves. Only that asshole Giuseppe was my father's spy, and off came the belt again. 'But no one forgot you,' Carmela told me, 'none of us, you were always in our hearts, especially because the older we got the more we understood, and we also used to talk about you to Francesco and even he began to love you.'"

"And you also started talking with your mother?"

"Even with my mother. Of course it was difficult pulling the words out of her mouth, I really needed to ask her a bunch of questions, she was … how shall I put it?"

"Reticent."

"Reticent? I wish! She was mute, silent as a tomb! She started to answer me, then she started crying. But I wanted to know everything, the details, and she: I don't know. I don't remember. Don't make me remember. I shouldn't say anything because she's my mother, God rest her soul, but she got on my nerves. It was like slamming into a brick wall."

"But in the end, you did it…"

"I was too impetuous, in the beginning. Carmela, my oldest sister, was always telling me, 'Rosa you have to be patient. You have to go slowly. This is what our mother is like, she lives in her own world most of the time, she prays and prays and prays, and no one knows where her mind is. You must remember that our

Calabria is not like your America. A woman, in Calabria was a slave, treated no better than the African slaves were in your America. Just think of the weight she must bear, a boulder-sized burden...' I made a face, Fred, as if to say, *she* has a burden to bear? *She* has the weight of a boulder on her? But my sister gently caressed my head, telling me, 'I know my sister, I know, but remember she is just as much a victim as you.'"

It was difficult for Rosa to understand her sister's point of view. Her blood was boiling, she needed to cool off, to assuage that resentment she felt growing toward this woman: sure, it was her mother, but *mother* was only a word, an empty, insignificant word, her mother was a dead alcoholic American who had raised her, more or less, made her study, she was a real piece of work but there were also some moments of tenderness, her own way of showing of affection. This old woman, who complained and cried continuously and went on about how much she had suffered, was actually her mother only for a moment: the precise moment when she had abandoned her, when she sold her to another woman. And then she thought about her American mother again, how she had bought Rosa on a whim because she couldn't have children, how she had taken advantage of that destitute Calabrian family, of that Calabrian mother whose baby she had taken away with the arrogance of her money, and the tenderness for her dead American mother was transformed into hate, a resentment that was choking her and made her sick, Rosa wished that she wasn't dead so she could have slapped her with the back of her hand and could have rammed that cucumber sandwich down her throat. Rosa lay in bed, so torn up she gnawed on her pillow, overcome by such vivid, terrifying dreams that she woke up screaming, her chest on fire, so full of rage it made her eyes sting. And she thought about her fathers again. God damn them! My executioners, she thought. My mothers' executioners, she thought. This hatred made her sick, so sick, that she had to run to the bathroom to puke. God, she wanted them to burn in hell!

XXXIV

"But did you believe in God?"

"Um, Fred, my boy. Let's say that I believed in God, yes, because if not where would I have channeled all that hatred? My fathers had died, my American mother was dead, my Italian mother was half dead and anyway she was the least guilty of them all, the only one alive was God. I hated Him. I had to believe in Him so I could hate Him. There were no excuses for what He had done."

Alfredo looked at her, totally blown away. He looked around. Statues of Madonnas, crucifixes, holy pictures. The red pepper from the arrabbiata sauce was burning his mouth, so he gulped down a little more wine than he should have.

XXXV

Rosa stayed in Trieste for five years. For those five years she cleaned houses and staircases, restaurant kitchens and offices, perfected her Italian, albeit with a curious inflection which drifted between the Calabrian dialect spoken at home, the Triestine dialect and English, but, most importantly, she looked after her mother who had a stroke two years after Rosa's arrival.

As a result of the stroke her mother spoke less and less and seemed more like her old rag doll. But Rosa, even though the fragmented memories of her older siblings and her mother were at odds with each other's, ended up understanding her past. And then finally she understood something else which happened while she was staying there, by watching and listening to her siblings, "the deprivation, Fred, you have no idea of what poverty really means. And the hunger. And neither did I. Thank God, I never knew such hunger and poverty. But my mother, my father, my brothers and sisters all did."

Alfredo looked at her silently, with a full stomach, not sure if he should take a third cutlet or just go for the cannolis. He was beginning to guess how she had successfully come to terms with the hatred she had felt for her fathers, her mothers, God, and how she slowly allowed her heart to forgive. Forgiveness was necessary, if not she would go nuts, trying to find the rationale behind God's mysterious plans. God, she said, sees beyond what we do and acts according to principles we can't understand. Extreme poverty. God had spared Rosa from poverty. And hunger. Carmela said that hunger was a monster that had tormented them. God only knows how Francesco had survived, without milk, without anything, he was a little bag of bones. "Oh Rosa," Carmela used to say, "I don't even want to tell you what we were forced to eat, we were so hungry!"

Her father died a year after he had sold Rosa to the Americans, swallowed up by a storm, along with his boat and fishing nets, by a furious, violent ocean teeming with hatred. His body was never found. Since he was a very astute sailor, various stories proliferated: that at a certain point the ocean had materialized into some kind of a devil with enormous jaws and had devoured him, that his sense of guilt and the burden of poverty had tortured him to such a degree that he deliberately jumped overboard, that he wasn't really dead at all, that someone had seen him board a ship bound for New York, it was said that he had left to look for his daughter. Rosa didn't believe any of it for a second, but entertained the possibility to soothe her heartache. Giuseppe, Carmela and the others couldn't think about it anymore, their only source of income had dried up and hunger was torturing them. They all moved to Trieste, spent several horrific years there, but they started working, at the port and on the ships, but above all, they had helped each other: Carmela married Tullio, a tall kind guy from Istria, with the clearest blue eyes, Rosa was probably fondest of him more than anyone else, even though she didn't see him that often, but she felt his strong presence through the stories that Carmela and the others told her. Tullio was a kind of hero for all of them. He was the butcher, sometimes the steward, on the cruise ships. He was sometimes at sea for six months, he even went to South Africa as well as Australia. When he returned after these long trips, he brought home a bit of everything, hidden in huge suitcases that the customs agents sifted through, without ever flagging his bags, in exchange for a few packs of cigarettes, or nothing at all: the agents knew that seamen didn't make much money and no one dared say a word. Of the thousand stories he loved to tell about his trips, which were so fascinating to Rosa, Tullio often laughed at the one about the diminutive nun who came down to the docks like clockwork from the orphanage on the Carso, once the ships were in port, with a very large bag so she could fill it up with as much merchandise as possible. One time a young customs agent had the nerve to tell her that she was not allowed to do this: the petite sister flew into a rage, became a tigress, a volcano, a she-devil, and threatened to get him fired because *she knew people.*

When Tullio emptied the contents of his suitcases on the table, everyone's eyes shone brightly, mouths wide-open: frozen lobsters, chocolate, large cuts of meat, sometimes even toilet paper. Everything was divided equally between siblings and in-laws: Tullio and Carmela didn't even take so much as an extra little box of food for themselves. Rosa told me, "I grew up in America and this close kinship, this harmony shocked me. I mean, every day in America I saw marriages come apart at the seams, starting with my parents'. And now, now it's worse than ever. And that's not all. It's the distance, Fred. America is too big, a place where you can easily get lost in the shuffle. Take my Aunt Lisa, she knew nothing about her sister. If my father had not run off and died, and if my mother hadn't ended up in such dire straits, they probably would have never seen each other again, Aunt Lisa would have never met me and I would have never known my Uncle Jeffrey and my cousin Jonathan. And my children... well, that's another story which I've already told you about."

I asked her, "and this Giuseppe, how did he end up in Como?"

Rosa got all worked up, "that bastard. After a year he became a waiter on the cruise ships, he met a very rich girl, got her pregnant, married her and now he's the lord of the manor. As for his family, it's as if they don't even exist, he's never given anyone of us a penny. But I feel sorry for him. He's his wife's lackey, she tells him what to do and what not to do, and she forbids him to see his family. He's a modern day mameluke."

"And the other three sisters?"

"Flora married Piero, who was also a sailor and a cruise ship waiter, they have two very beautiful daughters. Lucia married Dino, a friend of Piero's, same work, two children. Maria married Enzo, an elementary school teacher, three kids. And you know what the most amazing thing is? All of them managed to get Francesco to study, he earned a degree in nautical engineering and now he's rich, but honest, Fred, because he has never for a minute forgotten where he came from and what he owes to those who helped him get there. He never got married, he was always too shy, and this is something that has always made us sad, as we're his older sisters, but such is life."

"But you, why did you come back to America?"

"Five years after I arrived in Italy, my mother died. I took care of her like…"

She stopped for a second, surprising herself. Alfredo smiled, "like a daughter?"

She also smiled, "exactly. Toward the end it made quite an impression on me how thin she had gotten and much she resembled my other mother to a tee. I held her hand while she was in bed, when she said the most nonsensical things, and sometimes I was no longer sure exactly which one I was with, my two mothers had morphed into the same person. At a certain point, in her delirium, she told me, 'go back to America, go back to America.' Then she died."

"And because of that you came back here?"

"Well, when this is the only advice that your mother has ever given you, especially on her deathbed, you have to take it, right?

But then, there were other considerations. My two sisters, Flora and Lucia, and their husbands, were finally able to leave home and be independent. While I was there Maria got engaged, got married and left the house right away. After my mother's death I stayed with Carmela and Tullio, who was almost never there, and little Francesco, in the meantime Carmela got pregnant. I managed to get Italian citizenship, thanks to the depositions given by my two sisters, but finding a job was extremely difficult. So, since I was really being supported by my sisters and I felt indebted to them, I helped my sisters, I helped them with the children, I cooked for them, I washed, I ironed, and I taught Francesco English. But it seemed to me that each one of them had started to go down their own paths toward the future, I couldn't even see mine with binoculars. Plus I really wanted to see Aunt Lisa and Uncle Jeffrey, since we had continued writing to each other for the entire five years. What can I say? I wanted to be in America again, to go home. In the end maybe this was why: after five years I still felt like a foreigner, a guest who had stayed there for a certain amount of time, like on vacation, but my life was somewhere else."

"And when you came back, you went to live with Aunt Lisa and Uncle Jeffrey, and then you met Arcoleo?"

"Not even six months after."

"And you envisioned your future with Arcoleo?"

"Well, yeah Fred, and don't be such a smart ass. Arcoleo was handsome, earned a good living and was very affectionate. He was crazy about me, what do you think? You had to see me at twenty-four years old, I hadn't had three kids yet: I was a flower. I was intelligent, Fred, Arcoleo showered me with roses and love and he told me things that you can't even imagine, he made me dream."

"Arcoleo?!"

"Yes, yes, Arcoleo… yeah, I know, I know, no sense looking at me like that, just look at how men change once they're married. Not Tullio though, not him. Not even my other brothers-in-law, when I really think about it. But Arcoleo, yes, he changed. But how could I have known? I never had any experience with men, only books, and then he shows up, promising me a comfortable life of love and children. What more does a woman want? At least, that's how I thought about it."

XXXVI

Alfredo had completed his course load in three years and in his fourth year he finished his thesis, in the meantime he had looked around, applying all over the States to universities that were looking for art history teachers. He got lots of feedback, had the initial interviews, but in the end he had nothing to show for all this effort. Once again the specter of going back to Italy loomed over him. The idea didn't sound so horrible after five years in America, but in Italy the economy was sluggish, there were no high paying jobs, the salaries were the lowest in Europe and the future prospects were dismal. America, even with all its problems and the economy going to the dogs, continued to hint at the possibility of guaranteeing him a very agreeable present and the dream of a brilliant future, pointing to thousands of opportunities, arousing his desire to create something awesome for himself and the pride of finding success. He needed to stay in America.

The name of his hope was Sciagarone. By now they had become friends, he wanted Alfredo to call him Vito and at a dinner with some other professors he insisted that they sing *O sole mio* together. Luckily Alfredo had already had three or four drinks, because after *O sole mio* he also sang *Malafemmina*, and Sciagarone was moved to tears. Everyone applauded, jubilantly, drunkenly, animatedly, contentedly. What a strange species, these professors! Four years before he was astonished at how American professors seemed so different from their Italian counterparts: they were much more open, informal, generous, impassioned, seemingly envy free. However, he had gotten to know the American university system truly from the inside out, much more than he had after attending an Italian university. There probably were Italian professors who were less strict and conceited than they had seemed when he was in his twenties, as he now recognized that behind their casual façade there were also the same hypocrisy, arrogance, and underhanded internal wars between American professors. At this dinner, for example, no one could have spotted any trace of ill will in the innocent demeanor of Henriette Blanc, petite, round and five months pregnant, an expert in Renaissance art, with a smile that would have disarmed Botticelli. She often spoke to him, encouraged him, gave him advice, discussed the book she was working on with him and, in turn, wanted to know what he was working on. She was every guy's dream, small eyes and a graceful mouth, but one day Sciagarone took him aside and told him, "Ragazzo, senti..." then, not up to continuing in Italian, he switched to English, "that Blanc woman. Don't confide in her too much. In fact, I wouldn't trust her as far as I could throw her."

Alfredo was crushed.

"Why not?"

"Because whatever you tell her she'll end up using against you someday."

"What do you mean?" Alfredo felt intimidated, because he had never seen him so serious, even worried.

"She hates you."

Alfredo tried to laugh – human psychology was a mystery to him, including his own, which was why he preferred nuances of color to nuances of the mind, and paintings to people – but suddenly he was sure that Sciagarone was right, certain that the Blanc woman hated him. He pretended to be shocked, which he should have been, but he had already figured things out, and what he felt was not as troubling as the regret and bitterness he harbored, "she hates me... maybe she doesn't like me, if I anything..."

"No, no, she really hates you. She's a real snake in the grass, that one. She has a previous history of hating people, you can't even begin to imagine... well, anyway, stay as far away from her as you can."

"But why does she hate me?"

"Because she hates me. Anyone who hates me, also hates you, don't you see? Academia is a filthy business, all politics and there's a lot of pettiness. A maggot's nest of mediocre parasites."

XXXVII

In any case, the time flew by and Alfredo saw the hopes of his American dream trickle away. He started making inquiries to see if it would be possible to extend the deadline for handing in his thesis, postpone the completion of his Master's degree and also get confirmation of his assistantship for another semester. But Sciagarone seemed doubtful, perplexed, and answered by grunting, so that Alfredo left his office, very worried. Then, one evening Sciagarone called him at home. This was strange since he had never done this before. He invited Alfredo to have breakfast with him at a Greek restaurant on Federal Highway, he said he had to tell him something important. Good news or bad? Alfredo asked him anxiously. "No, it's good news, but it depends on us." That night Alfredo didn't sleep, he opened the fridge one too many times, drank too many beers, having a tough time even swallowing a mouthful, got into his beat-up '89 Hyundai and crisscrossed Boca, from east to west, until he ended up back east on Ocean Drive and drove slowly along the coast, passing by the majestic villas on one side, the black, murmuring ocean on the other. He replayed everything in his head, it had all seemed like the most beautiful and fragile dream ever, all his years in America, the twenty degree below zero wind in Indiana that lacerated his face, leaving a class, easing his feet into snow boots, seeking refuge in the nearest bar to drink boiling hot coffee, and then there was Florida, green and hot, its long streets as smooth as a ballerina's legs, the moon nestled in the sky like a silver peacock in one of Whistler's paintings.

The next day Alfredo had a wicked migraine, Sciagarone was wearing shorts and a cotton golf jersey and his promising smile was as radiant as the morning sky. The sunlight, coming through the large glass windows, flooded the restaurant and fell softly on the light green tables, on the retro hairdos of the raven-haired young waitresses, on the old people who were wolfing down pancakes with maple syrup – everywhere. That morning was so luminous and that sky such a pale shade of blue as the light poured into the restaurant, almost wanting to have breakfast as well, so ebullient, and Alfredo looked at the shorts, the golf shirt and Sciagarone's smile, all these things were signs of a good omen, so Alfredo felt his heart galloping towards intense happiness, he felt that happiness was there for him – yes, yes, his temples were throbbing but he wasn't concerned, there was good news waiting for him, very good news, because the morning light, the azure blue sky and Sciagarone's smile couldn't lie to him, couldn't trick him, *they were there for him.*

They got comfortable, started to peruse the menu, but Alfredo was unable to decipher what was written on it and he wondered if Sciagarone realized that he was hanging on his every word, but Sciagarone enjoyed keeping him in suspense: Sciagarone was as calm as a man who was getting ready to play golf, behaved like a man who doesn't have to look for work. Alfredo closed the menu as if he had already decided what to order and stared at him, instead the older man's attention was riveted on the menu, his reading glasses perched on his nose, his mouth curled up. Since Alfredo first met him in Indiana, three years ago, Sciagarone seemed to have aged thirty years, he seemed like he was three hundred years old, a three hundred year old man, yet he in excellent shape.

"Ragazzo, senti…" he said in Italian, then, worn out by the effort it took, continued in English.

"Yes, Vito."

"I'm retiring."

Alfredo felt a pang in his heart, the blood drained from his face, then the feeling spread, ice-cold, from his mouth to his stomach, his chest, his arms, all over his body. The important good news was for Sciagarone, not for him. The pale blue sky and the morning sunlight were there for Sciagarone, not for him. He didn't know what to say, then murmured, "so young?"

"Well, I'm not all that young, you know…"

He didn't get the irony even though it was right in his face.

XXXVIII

The waitress arrived. She was probably very young and very sweet, with a small nose, but Alfredo didn't dwell on that, nothing registered with him anymore. She rattled off the day's specials, and Sciagarone was as chipper as a songbird and ordered a breakfast that would choke a horse. Alfredo hated all of this but, feeling like a dagger had been thrust in his back, ordered a coffee.

"Just coffee?" The waitress and Judas said in unison, then they both urged him to have something else, "there's really fresh moussaka and the mutton pie is a masterpiece," so Alfredo, wanting to cut the conversation short, said:

"A slice of cheesecake."

The waitress left, probably annoyed, and Sciagarone went on, "so, I'm retiring. I've had enough. I've been in academia for forty years. It's a wonderful life, don't get me wrong. Books, all expense-paid-trips, attending conferences around the world, and the students. Being around young people helps you stay young, you know…"

"Yes, I can see that."

"Oh, thanks. But how old do you think I am?"

Alfredo always answered this question by subtracting ten years from the age that the person actually looked. This time he subtracted twenty: "sixty."

He looked a tad disappointed.

"Sixty-two. But really I look even younger than sixty, today you're seeing me dressed like this and last night I drank a little too…"

"Yes, of course, but you once told me that your daughter was forty years old, so I guessed that you had to be at least sixty."

He brightened up again, relieved, "oh, right!"

The waitress returned. She served Alfredo his cheesecake somewhat disdainfully and then, smiling at Sciagarone like he was her wealthy grandfather, served him his eggs Benedict, spicy sausages, hash browns, French toast and waffles with chocolate sauce.

Alfredo picked at his pie, wanting to drown his sorrows in his coffee when Sciagarone, with a mouthful of food, glanced at him resolutely and said, "anyway, my boy, as I was saying, I'm going on a trip around the world with my wife. Six months here, six months there, then who knows? Europe, especially, Paris, the Louvre, Madrid, the Prado, Naples, the pizza – ah! But also Australia, you know, and then China, we'll see. My wife deserves it."

"Sounds great." But for Alfredo the rest of the world just meant Italy, and Italy meant competitive exams, eligibility lists for job placement, being at home with Mom and Dad. He was lost in his thoughts.

"But this is where you come in. Obviously there will be an available position in the department. And I want you to have it."

XXXIX

Suddenly the sun and the sky turned into amazingly good friends again, the restaurant a fine example of modern Greek architecture, those old people adorable, the waitress captivating and Sciagarone an affable, very rich, grandfather.

"But how do we go about it?" Stammered Alfredo.

"Well, the same way everyone else does. By law, they need to officially announce that there's an opening for an Assistant Art Professor, which you will apply for. Decidedly, there will be at least fifty other applicants from all over the country. Once we have examined the applications and considered everyone's qualifications – I won't tell you how boring that is – we, the faculty, will get rid of forty and we'll choose ten: that makes nine plus you. A little after Christmas these ten applicants will be required to attend the American Association of Teachers convention in Philadelphia, once there we'll interview each candidate."

All the American universities that have listed one or more available positions, no matter what the field, would be at this convention. This used to take place every year right after Christmas, always in different cities, then all those selected had to go to the predetermined city to interview with more professors, either at the hotel where the professors were staying or at the reception room as big as a stadium of the convention venue (which usually was a large hotel as well). Hundreds of small, white, numbered tables were placed in the room, one for each university, and the candidates, once they located the university that had granted them an interview, went, at the appointed time, to be tortured by enigmatic questions such as: "but why do *you really* want to work at *our* university?" (Because you're the only one that called me back – was definitely not the right answer), "but how do *you* see *your* future?" (How should I know, I'm no Nostradamus – not the best way to answer either). The year before, in San Diego, Alfredo had received a notification to interview with a college in Texas and a university in Kansas, but any hopes were snuffed out after the interviews, so he consoled himself by eating quesadillas and getting shit-faced on tequila in the Mexican part of town.

XL

"But since I'm already here, can't they interview me in Boca?" Asked Alfredo.

"No, all the applicants must be treated exactly the same. We're in America, not in Italy."

"And after Philadelphia, then what happens?"

"We eliminate seven candidates, then we call you and two others back for the Super Bowl."

"What?"

"The Super Bowl, the grand finale, for the interviews on the campus."

Alfredo had heard about this. It was an unnerving process. Each finalist was invited, at the expense of the university, to visit the campus for two days. During these two days you had to jump through all kinds of hoops which were especially nerve-racking, acrobatics and circus acts, expending an indeterminate amount of smiles and strained laughter. In fact, it boiled down to a series of interviews which were meant to be courteous and, all in all, informal, but in the end it resulted in the applicant being bombarded with questions: psychological probing trying to discover your true soul, which essentially meant that everyone wanted to get one thing straight – were you a ball-breaker or not?

You had to spend a half hour with the college president or several administrators (who filled your head with a jumble of numbers hinting at your eventual contract) then with the department head, who pointed out various campus buildings, then with a plethora of select students, then with your possible future colleagues with whom you went to lunch – and you wondered if they were also there to analyze the food you chose and the way you brought it to your mouth. The most precarious part of the whole procedure was teaching a class to students you had never met before, who in turn stared at you inquisitively, while, at the back of the classroom, seated in a circle, were the judges, possibly your soon-to-be colleagues, whom you already vehemently hated, even more so when you caught glimpses of them taking notes on the way that you interacted with the students or trying to determine whether your blackboard penmanship was legible. Before these same judges, toward the end of the day, when you had a splitting headache and the judges couldn't wait to go home, and they couldn't possibly be as sharp as they were earlier in the day – and the last thing that they wanted to do was listen to an academic presentation – you had to present a research paper, followed by more questions. Finally, a limousine arrives, brings you to the airport where you start thinking that you want nothing more to do with this farcical, make-believe life, that you only want to go back to Italy and learn how to be a farmer.

"The problem, as usual, is that Blanc woman. She would kill herself rather than see you get the job, and she will look for allies to go up against you," said Sciagarone chewing.

"So, what do we do?" Asked Alfredo worriedly.

"Well, first of all you must realize that the Department Head position is quite a desirable one, and that they have to decide on a new Department Head before deciding on whom they want to entrust with the new job of Assistant Professor."

"Damn, but when they decide on filling the new opening you'll already be gone, you'll be as worthless as the two of spades!"

Alfredo realized that he had gone too far, caught up in the emotion, and Sciagarone turned as red as the ketchup bottle. Sitting there in his golf shorts, his face dotted with mayonnaise, he acted like a little snot whose feelings had been hurt, "no, no… the two of spades… look, *my* influence over these people will prevail even if I go live with the pygmies in Borneo… you have to understand that I've made a name for myself! Maybe because you're looking at me dressed like this … but an approving or disapproving nod of my head is all that's needed because tomorrow these people may or may not find a job in another university, might or might not publish their damned books…"

The look in the old man's eyes was unsettling, but Alfredo knew how to stroke his ego to restore his wounded pride, "sorry, but since I see you so often I sometimes forget that you're a celebrity."

The mere mention of the word celebrity instantly jolted Sciagarone back into a good mood again, he jabbed his knife into what was left of the sausage, brought it to his lips and ate it all in one mouthful, as if it were that Blanc woman. Chewing voraciously, he went on, "in fact, my input – like a king choosing his successor – counts a lot. Now, there'll be two candidates, Dr. Blanc and Wilson. And I will certainly not support Dr. Blanc, especially since that would kill you, but Wilson…. Wilson is a faithful lapdog and he likes everything I like, so he'll like you too, he'll cover your ass."

"And if Wilson, as head of the department, chooses me for the newly vacated position, no one would dare contradict the new department head, right?"

"Not with the same intensity as before. It's always better not to make an enemy of the Department Head. Besides, I'll still be around, in spite of my retirement, I'll always be part of the faculty and it won't do anyone any good to deny me a favor, I told you…" he chuckled gleefully, his eyes beamed joyfully, just thinking of his power.

"But you're sure that Dr. Blanc doesn't have a chance?"

She was young, admired, determined, had already published a significant amount of her work and wasn't afraid of Sciagarone, or at least it seemed like she wasn't – but Alfredo didn't mention that.

"Oh, whatever slim chance she has, we'll quash it: you see, Dr. Blanc is pregnant. And I will stall the crucial selection meeting for choosing the new Department Head right up until our dear Henriette is in the hospital having her baby."

XLI

Alfredo got the job, fifty thousand dollars a year, plus benefits, from August to May, with three weeks vacation at Christmas, summers off and, since it was a *tenure-track position*, if he did what he needed to do – that is publishing a few nebulous articles in literary reviews that no one ever reads and sitting on more diverse committees to discuss various goals that they would never attain – within seven years the professorship would be his and no one could force him out. His life was unfolding before him, beautifully and easily, carefree and stress free (except for the drama with Mrs. Blanc and his nights with Strauss). He could travel, read, fall in love, maybe even with a Mexican girl, perhaps he might even yield to the temptation of painting. He was extremely happy, fully aware of his good luck which he thought was all due to God's sense of guilt because He had created someone so lazy and inept. "Because I always knew that I was a loser," he said to me one evening when we had had way too much to drink, "I always knew that I didn't have the nervous energy to leave behind the sheltered world that my family, my education and my art had built around me. Away from the pampering I would have freaked out, away from the coddling, in what they call the real world, the ways of the world would have destroyed me." "It seems to me that you'll muddle through it once you're with people," I told him, pumped up by a sense of male bonding, intensified by the wine, and yet I was being sincere. But he came back with, "sure, I'll always get by, being with people. The fact is that, since I would be embarrassed if the world figured out my true personality, I've cultivated an aura of sociability, a sense of humor and even a certain swagger, so that very few people, I think, would suspect my ineptitude. Strauss, for one, doesn't suspect it. But I know very well that I'm a loser and God, or whoever was standing in for Him, must have felt some sense of guilt by creating me like this and to rectify the situation He allowed every stumbling block to crumble away, put the angel Sciagarone on my trajectory, He let me be coddled."

Several months later Alfredo had become an Assistant Professor and Rosa was made the manager of the cafeteria Burger King: one day Alfredo felt like having a decent hamburger and French fries, Rosa glanced down at his shoes and recognized him as a fellow countryman. There was a twenty-year age difference between them, they were leading totally opposite lives but they became friends and out of the blue Rosa told her story to Alfredo, who asked his friend for her permission to tell me her story because I wanted to get it down on paper – it seemed to me that it was an emotionally charged story, one that deserved to be written.

XLII

What astonished Alfredo the most was that no one had ever asked Rosa for forgiveness. Not her American mother, not her Italian mother, not the innkeeper, not her brothers and sisters, no one. But one day, one calm and crisp day, as ethereal as a tender caress at the end of winter, finishing their cigarettes, while gazing up at the sky, Rosa said to him, "Fred, you'll never guess who I dreamed of last night."

"Who?"

"God."

"God? You mean Jesus?"

"No, no it *was* God. Beside, Fred, Jesus *is* God."

"How can you dream about God? What was He like? Did He have a white beard?"

"No."

"Did He come out of a cloud, in a burst of light?"

"I don't know… It's hard for me to explain… I can't find the right words."

"It's plausible. There have been some famous precedents. But do you at least remember what He said to you?"

"Yes. He asked me to forgive Him."

Alfredo didn't budge, remaining as immobile as a piece of stone, like Rosa's childhood house.

"And what did you do?"

"What was I supposed to do, Fred?"

Alfredo looked at her, saw that light in her eyes, which reminded him of his little town in Italy, then heard her whisper, "I forgave Him."

The Complete Works of Ellery Queen

I was wandering between the tables at an outdoor café in Delray Beach, thinking about the vanity of mankind, when all of a sudden I saw this huge black woman, dressed in purple and orange, who was reading a tiny yellow book, a detective story. Ah, if only I had been born a painter!

(I'm not saying a Raphael or a Mantegna, even a second rate painter, a minor Lithuanian from the last century – I would call the painting: "Large Black Woman With Murder Mystery").

It was one of those cafés and one of those mornings from a bygone Florida, both suspended in the opalescent heat of the sun, in the azure-blue incandescence of the sky, with the sound of the ocean breathing calmly across the street, a half mile farther away, the shrill delightfully ear-splitting droning of the cicadas and the indistinct squawking of the seagulls. On those mornings the smell of sausages and eggs drifts out of busy restaurant kitchens and blends in with the aroma of suntan lotion and gasoline and everything, cars, human beings and iguanas, don't seem to be in a hurry, they seem like part of the scenery, like the asphalt cracked from the sun or the shrubbery.

I liked that place, I like watching people, their features: such as the burnished skin of that Peruvian guy with a large nose, his eyes full of nostalgia. That old lady, once very beautiful, who still emanates flashes of her former beauty while, engrossed in the New York Times, she nibbles on her buttered bread. That guy with the potbelly, in the straw hat, white beard, khaki shirt and Bermuda shorts, who gingerly takes a cigar from his pocket, thinking he's someone else. You know, in Florida everybody believes he's someone else.

But I immediately understood that the large woman was somehow different, she was amazing, I couldn't take my eyes off her. I tried to get closer to her, to do something so she'd notice me, I banged into a couple of tables, stared earnestly at the tiny book, without getting a rise out of her, she was indifferent, an ebony statue on the Atlantic coast in the Delray sunshine, a goddess, her brow furrowed. But I know how to be persistent and finally, without even looking up from her tiny book, barely arching her eyebrow – the right one, I believe – she murmured (in superb English that floored me), "what do you want, get lost." I had distracted her from reading.

But I was smitten. I was admiring her feet imprisoned in her worn-out slave sandals, her African queen's hands, her delicately manicured fingernails like tigers' claws, as sharp as cut diamonds, her imperious expression, terrifying, and not even a trace of mascara!

I felt the sun burning my skin, I felt my head burning, I inhaled all the smells, the aroma of the salt air, the fish, the mangoes, the dust from the street, I saw all the colors, the blue from the sky and the red from the flowers and the yellow lines of the crosswalk – you know how it is when you fall in love.

I couldn't back down. I stayed where I was, my eyes welling up, something that works with women. She looked at me, she seemed contemptuous of me, but I knew that I had gotten to her, come on mamma stop pretending, come on mamma, we're all alone and you know it!

She put the tiny book down on the table and with her delicate forefinger – the left one, I believe – she gestured for me to come closer.

She asked me several questions which I preferred not to answer.

She thought I was stupid, everyone did, but it didn't matter to me, I hopped into her pink Cadillac and we went cruising on Ocean Boulevard.

Our love story began like this. Other people, certainly, didn't call it love, they said we kept each other company, with a couple like that you can't talk about love. But it was really love, a love made up of little things, a love that other people would not have dreamed of and didn't dream of, poor fools, vain braggarts, they know nothing about the love that we had when at night, silently, on a green velvet couch, side by side we watched our friend the TV, the Food Channel and old John Wayne movies, when, arm in arm we went beddy-bye in your large bed, and when in the morning your first smile was for me and mine was for you. What do they know about the love that was in an insignificant gesture, insignificant to other people, when you cooked fried catfish for me and prepared it with such care, deboned and unsalted, that it tugged at my heartstrings and I ate all of it with tear filled eyes because of your kindness, your generosity, because I loved you so very much and I didn't want to let you know that I never liked catfish.

And how well we settled into our little house! You called it your dump, but believe me, there's a lot worse. The curb appeal of the house detracted from it: it needed a coat of paint, all the white paint was peeling off the wood, corroded by the fierce sunlight and the August rains, and the mailbox, misshapen from rust, seemed like an old stuffed flamingo, but the purple front door made me feel happy. You had no inclination to garden either: facing the back patio, the messy yard grew, neglected, the wooden picket fence was rotting and the underbrush grew straggly between pieces of glass and spare metals parts from cars, nor were you worried that it had become a home for snakes and other pleasant critters. But, on certain gold tinged evenings in October, before dinner, you liked to flop onto the old rocking chair on the patio, wearing only a light white nightgown, reading one of your thousand novels. I was next to you, watching you and hearing you boast, "for the most part these books are so pedestrian, idle musings, worthless fodder or pot luck, like dumping buckets of paint on a canvas to see what you get. All literature is a joke."

I didn't understand you. But the fact that you shared your opinions with me was enough to make me feel blessed, while the little blue clouds above us let themselves be gently pushed along by gusts of wind, so very slowly, like two freeloaders in a carriage.

You were proud of your library. Bookcases and bookcases made of lightly colored wood, full of books, books masterfully arranged according to the color scheme of the books' spines, it went from the snobbish white of Elizabethan sonnets to the well-worn green of the spy stories to the frolicking fuchsia of the novels set in New York, full of whiskey and beautiful women, to the dusty black of old editions of the Greek tragedies. There were books whose covers were creased, with damaged spines, some torn off and worn-out, books marked by circular stains of wine and coffee (you always put your cup or your wine glass on the book when you went to the bathroom), notations in red and insults for the author, graceful doodling with curlicues on the edges of the pages, like illuminated medieval miniatures, books smudged with greasy fingerprints, with the pages stuck together from squashed bits of French fries, deluxe editions with short recipes scribbled on the first page (you often used to read with the TV tuned in to the cooking shows). But what you were most proud of, as you repeatedly told me, was a set of *The Complete Works of Ellery Queen*, dark yellow, stretched out like a hammock between a pale brown volume of Saint Augustine and an ochre colored collection of essays by Baldwin.

One day we took the pink Cadillac and we went off to the wedding of I don't exactly remember whom, one of your distant cousins I believe, in North Carolina. How proud I felt, my beloved buxom beauty, when you finally introduced me to your family! (It was time that you did).

It was an incredible wedding, everyone as black as the ocean on a tropical moonless night. Everyone had bright white teeth and wore gold rings, I thought they would treat me disinterestedly, the racial question you know, and instead everyone smiled at me, everyone was nice to me and they offered me loads of hush puppies and fried catfish from an awesome buffet.

In my opinion it was also because of fried catfish that you didn't wake up one morning, you seemed to be finally sleeping peacefully, a little smirk on your face, your lips half-closed: I watched over you for three days so that no one would dare to wake you up, but I knew that you would not wake up, I'm not as dumb as they think. I knew it and out of desperation and hunger I devoured *The Complete Works of Ellery Queen* and in the end I shrieked in pain when they came to take you away. I followed them, now silently, and I saw, I saw everything you know, I saw them put you in a casket and then put it in a hole in the ground with a black stone on top of the grave. You wouldn't have liked that black stone at all, but at least I can crouch down all day and place an ear there – the right one, but sometimes even the left one – so I can hear if you're still talking to me, I can wait for night-time, dreaming about sleeping with you again, then waking up and looking up at the moon, and howling.

Portrait in Green With Proust

There was a time when Alfredo Crepuscolo wore a green hat. He went into a yellow bar and looked around. Captivating couples were drinking Martini & Rossi red vermouth mapping out the best strategy for their Saturday night plans. Jazz riffs were wailing from the sound system, the lighting was subdued and hazy: the smoke from Egyptian cigarettes filled the semi-darkness.

Alfredo took it all in, somewhat disdainfully, with that hard-assed look of his. There was a guy wearing a bottle green colored shirt holding hands with a bleached blond, who was distractedly looking off somewhere else. There was a babe with a ring in her nose and a dude with a ring in his ear, a girl who was crying and a guy who was always laughing. What a collection of wimps, Alfred thought. But no one cared. Then he got comfortable on a very high bar stool.

"The usual" he said to the bartender.

"The usual? I've never even see you before."

The bartender had a black mustache, black hair parted on the side, dark spiral snail shells for eyes and was obviously well out of the closet. He resembled Marcel Proust. Alfredo asked him:

"Excuse me, but do you live in a cork padded room?"

"Come again?"

"Forget it, it's not important, I'll have a Cuba Libre on the rocks. Make it a double."

Then, all of a sudden, *she* came in, draped in fuchsia, like a brick thrown through a plate glass window, an explosion in the night, two scintillating legs shining like a group of knights whose armor glitters in the sunlight, her perky breasts as robust as a regiment of infantrymen. But that Alfredo Crepuscolo, what a man of impeccable character! Such sublime indifference! He took out his lighter, lit a cigarette, adjusted the brim of his green hat

and was about to wave to her. There was a lingering look between them, he threw down the gauntlet, felt a stabbing pain in
the chest and Alfredo Crepuscolo almost toppled head first off
his bar stool. She slid her arm between her escort's, she was still a
knockout.

Was this for real? He would have liked to ask Proust, but he
would have gone off on the tangent. Rebecca. The lighting was
opaque, the couples were whispering sweet nothings in each other's ears and the music was just music. Rebecca. High cheek-
bones, melancholy, she resembled a stork, her hair the color of
wheat in August, her eyes a tropical green flecked with shades of
brown: ash and wetlands, emeralds and green tobacco. Even a
touch of madness. That strain of green, Rebecca! Rebecca. A
staccato name, one that dealt you a real blow. A name like a Ni-
belung. What do you think, Marcel?

But Marcel was dilly-dallying, vigorously sloshing the ice
around in the rum, thinking about the fact that the cities we long
to be in take up much more relevant space in our lives than those
where we actually end up. A beautiful thought, Marcel.

Rebecca sat down at a small table near the combo, on a small
green couch. It was marble green, marine sediment green. Nothing but a sea of green. Marcel, who's in charge of the décor here,
the Tree Hugger Party?

Rebecca's dapper date sat next to her, the guy was solidly
built, wore a double-breasted suit and his eyes sparkled with ne-
farious shades of grey: a *homo economicus*, no doubt. He placed
his hand on her stocking covered knee. Oh Rebecca, you're such
a coward! I'm the only one who had the right to touch that knee,
remember? I used to kiss it like it was a jewel, oh that knee, oh
that nubile knee! But does one kiss precious stones? Alfredo,
you've read too many insipid, saccharine poets, believe me.

But the fact was that Rebecca was right there, in front of him,
and she was letting this boorish guy caress her knee with his
sweaty hand, while she stared at Alfredo the whole time. And the
look on her face! It betrayed all the passion of their days together,

all the anger and regret, and the tenderness, oh Rebecca, Rebecca! How long has it been? Ten years, twenty, a hundred, it was
yesterday. It was only yesterday that you told me… what did you
say to me?

"I'm begging you, begging you, don't ever leave me."

(The impossibility of remembering burned just like the rum,
because there had been a time when she had meant everything to
him, and he had meant everything to her, oh yes, thousands of
embraces had kept them almost soldered together, bound to an
adolescence that was vaporizing around them, thousands of kisses and now not even a taste of one left, thousands of words rehearsed before a mirror, performed for only one spectator, her,
so refined, so sincere, thousands of promises made while the future devoured it all, thousands of promises not there anymore,
the rum slid smoothly down his throat and soon there was nothing more to remember, only Rebecca looking at him, right now,
and some idiot sitting next to her.)

Then it happened, she got up to use the Ladies' Room. Her
stockings rustled like a hissing serpent. Just as she was about to
disappear into the bathroom, she turned and shot him one last,
prolonged glance, an invisible bridge of smugness. Alfredo
turned to stone, breathless. He had to move. He just had to. He
fiddled with his green hat, cocked it at a rakish angle, slipped off
his stool, went by the meticulous metrosexual with the frightening eyes and stood near the restroom door.

He was cold and heard the pounding of a drum, but it was
his heart. He would grab her as soon as she exited the bathroom,
take her in his arms and kiss her on the lips without saying anything, and they would leave the club, pass by her bimbo boyfriend, who would make quite a racket and looked like an idiot in
his double-breasted suit, he would swear profusely at Alfredo
and try to punch him out, but Alfredo would punch him in the
nose or else he'd poke him in the eye with his finger or they'd

surreptitiously escape like thieves in the night – it didn't matter! Right now he had to kiss her, just kiss her, and the night would be theirs, and she would be his again, forever.

The door opened.

Alfredo's pulse was racing.

There she was.

"Hey" she said calmly, a little embarrassed by the look on his face.

"H… Hey," he stammered.

But she wasn't blond.

She had red hair styled as if she were an adolescent boy. And she didn't have green eyes. Not tobacco green or emerald or wet-lands' green and there were no specks of ash. She was wearing jeans and a chamomile colored t-shirt and said, "excuse me." Alfredo followed her with his eyes and she sat down where Rebecca had been sitting before, next to her Dapper Dan, but he wasn't all that stylish, he was a little guy with ginger hair, baggy pants and dopey looking blue eyes.

Dammit, Alfredo thought, I was wrong, it wasn't Rebecca.

Relieved and feeling a little down in the dumps, Alfredo took out a cigarette and started to think about appearances. Then he went back to the bar, sat on the same stool and asked Proust for another Cuba Libre. But Proust wasn't paying even the slightest bit of attention to him. He was caught up in a conversation with a gangly guy wearing a hat similar to his own, his mustache darted out like two syringes, he was wearing round glasses and he had wild eyes. He was speaking Gaelic, changing topics without skipping a beat. But look, whom do we see, James Joyce!

Alfredo looked at him and he almost felt like laughing, normally he would have been happy to hang out and shoot the shit, but it was late, his mother was still up, waiting for him to come home, besides he didn't know what to say, he had no theory on his remembrances of thing past, the band was wrapping up for the night, the last customers were fleeing like vampires, a new day was dawning with its sordid obligations. He'd have to wait for another night to enjoy the lights and the music, but Alfredo Crepuscolo still had his green hat on, so he pulled it down just so, and left.

A Season In Florida

It's not that I wouldn't like to stick my hand between Cristina's legs. No, no. I'd really like to. It's just that Cristina is Helen's daughter and Helen is a student of mine, even though Helen's twenty years older than I am, I'm almost thirty-three, she's almost fifty-three, has topaz green eyes, used to be a jazz singer, has suddenly decided to go back to college, and she's quite a fox with those perky round tits of hers. Not that I wouldn't also like to shove my hand up Helen's legs, but she is my friend, as is her husband Jeffrey, plus she is my student, I can't hook up with my students – it's in my contract – can you imagine if I started screwing the daughters of my students!

But in any case I had dinner at their house tonight, and Cristina was there, her eyes, rimmed with kohl, made her look like a Phoenician princess, her dark eyes were imbued with melancholy, the perplexing melancholy of twenty year olds, the baffling beauty of twenty year olds, she had a glass of wine in one hand and a book in the other, and was stretched out on the cream colored sofa, barefoot, then she put down the wine glass and called who knows whom on her phone and started to read passages from the book to this person.

Meanwhile I got to know the other guests, Helen was speaking very bad French, since some of the guests were French, and we all talked about how we missed, not so much Italy or France, but Europe, that damp humid smell of its churches and bricks, the cafés in the town squares and other inanities – but I was thinking about Cristina. She had incomparably delicate feet, tired, bruised bronze feet, and her leather sandals, that she had kicked off, were on the carpet making me sappily sentimental, I wanted to pick them up and kiss them, and then kiss her feet, lick them and then dry them with my three day old beard.

Instead I stood there arching my eyebrows at these two Frenchmen (if there's a nationality that irks the shit out of me, it's definitely the French) and I was knocking back wine from the lush green California vineyards saying that Marseilles seemed a little like Naples, even though I had never been to either place. And then I caught sight of her, we were standing in the spacious kitchen preparing salads and spreading paté on slices of toasted baguette, and Jeffrey – Helen's athletically toned husband – was barbecuing by the side of the pool, meanwhile Cristina was in the large living room, still on the phone reading excerpts from this book, she was wearing jeans and a white blouse, her black hair made her look like a Grecian goddess, her suntanned feet were marked with thin white strips left by the sandals straps, and she resembled an Athenian who had run all the way from Marathon to announce the Greek victory over the Persians and had just collapsed on the finish line.

We dined very well at their house and, besides myself, Cristina, Helen and Jeffrey, there was their old fart Uncle Lou, the French couple and the guy's son from a previous marriage, a little fourteen-year-old kid who played up having lost his mother when he was ten, acting like a real pain in the ass, rude to Helen ("the salad dressing is horrendous") and as haughty as a ballerina from La Scala.

God, I really hate kids. At a certain point, the conversation drifted to a pathetic story of a couple of famous actors who had lost a daughter, and Helen made a very astute comment about how devastating it is to loose a child, and I said "depends on the child." Then Cristina, who was sitting next to me, started laughing so exuberantly that my stomach muscles contracted and she inadvertently banged her foot – she was still barefoot – into mine, and then I inhaled all the perfume emanating from her body, and I wanted her lips, I pictured her standing against the garage door, giving in completely, moaning because I was sliding my hand between her legs and rubbing her pubes, oozing her white love juices, and, I don't know why, I had this image in my mind of starting to do the twist while I'm getting her off with my fingers.

Enough wine, I said to myself.

I started to talk, I get it that this is Helen's daughter, I hoped that Helen hadn't noticed, I was lonely and confused and her daughter's eyes were as dark as an Arabian night and her feet were as sublime as those of an Egyptian deity, I asked her "what are you reading?"

I got lost in that look of hers, as she was in mine, women have always found me alluring, and she became all flustered when I asked about the book, she got up suddenly to get it, and I watched this twenty year old girl stand up with such poise, and I become one with the earth and the stones, I belonged to mankind, I belonged to the fire of the world, oh what a precious moment happiness is! She got up and her ass was regal, languid, an ass to nibble on and fall asleep on, she had the ass of a Persian queen, and just at the moment Uncle Lou pounced on me.

Uncle Lou is the typical, stand-up old American guy, deaf and patriotic. He has enormous eyes hidden behind two inch thick glasses, makes very tasty cocktails and believes that America has always done so much good for the world and has received diddly-squat in return, that we should bomb the Middle East, China and Korea, and he still gets all choked up remembering the A-bombs dropped on Nagasaki and Hiroshima. But the one I adored nodded at me with a smile that pierced my flesh, I said my goodbyes to uncle Lou and the rest of the group telling them I was being summoned to the sofa, I got up respectfully, and approached her. I sat down practically glued to her thin, lithe little frame. "Here's the book," she said, and smiled, really smiled, her ruby red lips were dewy, she had an ancient past buried in those eyes, and her sandal free feet were golden, gleaming like camellia leaves, and I wasn't sure if all that enthusiasm was for me or for the book she was reading, "it's a life-changing read," she said, "it's expanding my mind," she said, and I read the title: *The Path of Being.* Subtitle: *How to Channel Positive Energy And Chase Away*

Negativity. It sent shivers down my spine. The fascination for everything that I find revolting made me forget about Cristina for a moment, she was talking and saying such nonsensical things expressing her admiration for the book, then she got up all of a sudden, her mother had asked her to make coffee. I sat all alone on the couch, I turned the book over and on the back dust jacket was a photo of the author, a what's-his name with yellow tinged skin, eyes like a hyena and a scraggly beard, who thought himself a "Spiritual Teacher" and who, in the aftermath of the international success of the aforementioned book, translated into 15 languages, toured the world to "teach about the soul". I couldn't resist, I started to read the preface. The jaundiced looking what's-his-name, a guy around my age, claimed to have been a manic-depressive with suicidal tendencies, but one night, at the height of his desperation, the Truth was revealed to him, which was we must liberate ourselves from our Ego ("nothing more than an illusion of our mind which prevents us from living in the moment") so that Energy flows into our lives and makes us aware of our Being.

The book explains exactly how to do this, and this jaundiced looking what's-his-name is a millionaire. This is not that astonishing to me. The world is full of these characters who fill the voids in other people's lives with their own brand of bullshit. The fact is we still don't understand this paling of our emotions, this sagging of our flesh, this death of someone whom we loved so much, this blinding loneliness, this pain gnawing at us like a bitter herb, this injustice we have to put up with, these careers to pursue, these hobbies to cultivate, these weekends by the ocean – and the inconsistencies are so strong that the bullshit is translated into 15 languages, and this made me feel empty too, desperately empty, and no amount of bullshit could appease me. Cristina sat next to me once again and I looked in her eyes, she was smiling and said "I'll lend it to you if you want" and I didn't know how to answer her, I was as cold as ice and mankind disgusted me, and I no longer felt like caressing her feet and now I understood why, while I was masturbating her in the garage with my fingers, I was doing the twist.

Tonight the Florida night was expansive and extremely hot, it's almost June and it seems as sticky as flypaper, and I can't go home, I had a cigarette and I felt the wine churning inside me, so instead of going home I went straight on Glades Road and ended up in some kind of disco.

God, I haven't been in a club since I was fifteen years old, and even then I felt out of place. There was a frightening mob of people, a confusing wave of humans immersed in darkness and smoke, everyone had about one square foot of space apiece, jumbled up like slaves in the cargo hold of a galleon, and on the stage there was a band making an indecipherable racket. A white female singer in a black miniskirt was screeching into a mike and the rhythm was monotonous like a hammer pummeling bleeding eardrums, but people were moving around, swaying their hips, rotating pelvises shoulders fists, shaking their heads. Then, some blond elbowed me in the side and I turned around, expecting an apology, but nothing, you don't have time to apologize in a disco, and so I kept going forward disentangling myself from a forest of arms and legs, I wanted to get to the bar and have a shot of whisky, then bam! Another elbow to the ribs. I turned around again for another apology, but zero, like it was nothing at all, all these people have elbows that don't feel anything, but the last guy caught my attention. He was an old man, about fifty-seven, the typical good looking fifty-seven year old guy, grey hair combed straight back, white shirt, cashmere sweater casually tied around his shoulders, linen pants, the typical fifty-seven year old divorcé with two kids somewhere else, a boy and a girl who have never forgiven him, and he was with a thirty year old who was in front of him, both of them had a good foot of space between them and – they were dancing.

Well, he was dancing, he was dancing up a storm (the thirty year old, not so much, she was nursing a drink) and the more the singer belted out that same obsessive beat, the more he flailed about and danced in every conceivable position rubbing his body up against the thirty year old's, badly simulating waltzes tangos mazurkas, arms outstretched, wiggling his ass, but what I found odd was the look on his face: he was concentrating so hard. He clenched his jaw, sucked in his cheeks, chewing on his lower lip, eyes closed as if the music were going into his body intravenously, as if *he could feel the beat* – as if he were young.

He was really pathetic looking and I felt absolutely disgusted by the sight of him, but I couldn't take my eyes off him. It was one of the most ridiculous things I'd ever seen. He was probably a very rich man, with a convertible, and the thirty year old was looking maternally at him – but he was fifty-seven years old pretending to be seventeen and that music meant something to him, and I felt embarrassed for him. My heart was filled with bitterness and I thought about all these people who filled the void in their lives with bullshit, and they had all come here, to be in this sweaty, sultry club, flailing about like monkeys to an obsessive rhythm and off-key screaming. It couldn't be they were enjoying themselves, it was scientifically impossible, but they needed to believe it, because it was Saturday night and on Monday it was back to work. This old idiot continued to move around like a primate in heat and I thought that if I kept staring at him he would say to me: "what the fuck are you looking at?" And then I would play dumb, I would stop daydreaming, I would apologize, smiling the whole time, saying that I was a little distracted – and in fact the old guy did ask me: "what the fuck are you looking at?"

And I gave him a truly awesome punch in the mouth, an exceptional belt, it was stupendous, and he fell like a sack of bananas, was bleeding right in the middle of the crowd, and other people fell like duckpins and I wriggled my way out of there as swiftly as a snake and in two minutes time I was in my car.

So this was how I spent my evening in Florida, but I'm sad and I'm thinking about Cristina and I think that maybe I could talk to her and explain to her that that book is pure bullshit, I could educate her, and I could love her and feel good and just enjoy her smile, because I crave beauty, I have a desperate desire for beauty, talent and beauty, and I need to be loved, I also need to be loved, by a girl who resembles an Athenian or even a cat, actually a cat is better, because the human race disgusts me.

Revelations

Revelations. In the span of an existence there are two or three, and invariably the second and third ones are love and death – but the first, the first is usually the sweetest. It's a hand, rough and filthy, fumbling between your legs.

It happened to Lud when he was twelve years old, a classroom, a young girl with thick, opaque glasses, that none of his young classmates ever paid any attention to. Too thin, too homely. Everyone focused on the Galbanini girl, her little melons already mature and as hard as granite, or Dolores decked out in burgundy miniskirts and already exposing pocks of cellulite, or little Fiammetta, who was easy and let anyone who helped her with her homework fondle her…

But not Francesca. She was a withered little daisy, a randomly assembled bag of bones, who wore sad colorful tights. When she smiled, her braces gave her a sinister luster. Sizing her up, a crappy poet might have the impression that premature death was looming over her and he would have attributed that same allure of fractured fragility to her that all the great bards had been infatuated with since the Thirteenth century….

So? Had the clairvoyant sensitivity of the young Lud sensed the radiant smile of beauty beyond this carapace of awkwardness? Or rather did he, being more base and insecure than his contemporaries, feel more at ease with Francesca's bony knees than with the other girls's precocious butts?

They were in the same row, both mediocre students both confused because of their physical inadequacies. They were in that section of the classroom – a minority to boot – who lived marginalized in the corner, not invited to parties, excluded from the thrills of childhood.

But it wasn't so much his exclusion that he regretted. Being an outcast, a child can write that off, can even brag about it, convincing himself that he's special, chosen by the gods, a superior being destined to accomplish great things. Yes, in a quasi-mystical melting pot you can overlook the fact that you're an outsider. The tears shed in a small bedroom or in the warmth of the bathroom, sitting on the toilet bowl, head in your hands, are ennobling, they hone individualism, and the child is already imagining becoming an adult when he can redeem himself. For now, go ahead laugh among yourselves. Someday *I* will be laughing, and it will be an unrelenting laughter. In the future *I* will be president of a very powerful multinational corporation and *you* will come and ask me for a job and I'll slam the door in your face and have you kicked out by security. In the future we'll meet again, sooner or later, at a school reunion, and we'll see who will end up with more in life. In the future you'll come and shake my hand and ask me for help and *I* will exclude you, and *you* will be the outsiders, *you* will be the outcasts…

It was not being an outsider that made him sad, even though there really isn't anything sadder in the world than a child playing all alone. In the silence of solitude, his imagination filled the void – but oh, how hard it is to be left out of the crowd! How hard it is not to have any friends at twelve years old, a time when you consider friendship the most important thing! And most of all, how hard it is to be left out of the dalliances when no sun seems more dazzling than Galbanini's smile. And yet I'm repeating myself again, it wasn't so much the exclusion that he regretted. It was the constant humiliation: Tom creeping up close to him like a lizard and doing a boorish imitation of his voice, Tom, in front of Galbanini and Dolores, saying, "Hey little faggot voice". And Galbanini and Dolores laughing. They laughed scornfully. They even patted Tom on the back, congratulating him. Ah, how could they be so cruel? Human nature is really malicious and children whose humanity has not yet been tempered by reason (by morality!) are the meanest of all. The little group walks away sneering, but their laughter is like splinters sticking into every part of his flesh while he just sits awkwardly next to

Francesca. I see him sitting there and it seems to me that he's been wounded by arrows like Saint Sebastian, or even crucified like Jesus, and giving him a drink from the vinegar soaked sponge was not a centurion but Galbanini: Galbanini how could you?

There's one obvious difference. Saint Sebastian and Jesus are tragically, extraordinarily handsome. Lud is 4'11", and has a zit on his forehead.

Don't think that the comparison is over the top. Every day Lud lives out the aforementioned episode. Since he's so small he would never have the audacity to react, and telling someone who might be able to fix the problem (his parents, a teacher) would seem even more humiliating to him. Asking an adult for help would mean confessing his own dilemma of being a child, and especially of being a weak child. It's a dead end. He doesn't sleep at night and going to school in the morning is like facing a firing squad, reliving in his mind, hundreds of times, the scenario that he regularly endures. When Tom gets sick and doesn't come to school, Lud feels like he has been spared by a miracle, as if the entire firing squad missed the target: Lud's only wish is to see Tom dead. Don't get me wrong, it's not because he hates him. It seems strange, but his fear of Tom is so invasive that there is no room for any other emotion, even the most natural one of revenge. He wants Tom dead because it seems like the only solution for him to live peacefully.

He is so terrified and in such pain because of the scene that repeats itself with disarming regularity, that not only does he not have time to hate Tom, he doesn't even have the time to hate Dolores, or Galbanini.

The pain of humiliation is the only sure thing. Nietzsche found the idea of eternal recurrence devastating, and Lud would have understood this very well. You don't get used to the pain, the pleasure loses substance through repetition, the pain is always the same, gritting its teeth each time it returns. So it's obvious that being an outcast – forgotten, ignored – became a much better option for him than staying there subjected to Tom's acrimony, and to the hysterical laughter, like knives, from Dolores or Fiammetta, and to Galbanini's shrill whinnying...

But Lud, why don't you react once and for all? Why don't you respond, you don't answer back, at the risk of having the shit kicked out of you by Tom? Better to die once, than live in terror forever...

But Lud hadn't even thought about this. If the pain is repeated every day, it hurts the same way, but what happens is that you think *that's life*. That's the way it is and there are no other alternatives. So the pain is the same, but it doesn't surprise us anymore. It terrifies us, but no longer surprises us. We scream the first time, eyes bulging, because we don't understand the absurdity of it, the rest we suffer in silence, because we have understood that pain is *always* absurd. The element of surprise is gone.

It was because of this that one day, while Lud-Saint Sebastian-crucified Christ was sitting silently, Francesca's words were a revelation:

"Don't get all bent out of shape, he's an imbecile," Francesca reassured him, smiling compassionately, as she always did, and in her empathy there was sensitivity of a common anguish.

Lud tried to laugh.

"What are you talking about? I'm not upset at all, I know he's joking... Tom is like that."

"And he's pretty homely. His nose looks like an elephant's trunk."

Like a bucket of water waking you up from a nightmare.

Like the apple on Newton's head.

Like having the mask of reality removed in a second.

"What?"

"His nose. You never noticed that nose?"

"Well... it's true..." Lud looked at Tom and he saw him for the first time.

Large, gigantic, horrendous. And that moron with that hideous honker on *his* face has the balls to make fun of *my* voice???

My voice will change, I'll get taller, but that nose will always be there – the despicable badge of his stupidity!!!

From that moment on he truly hated Tom.

"He's got a big nose, eh?" Lud repeated, seeking solace.

"A real schnoz!

"A real schnoz!!!" Lud laughed excitedly, and kept repeating, "a huge nose, a real schnoz!!!"

They both laughed, accomplices, with that amazing revelation.

It was at that moment, for the first time, that he wanted to kiss her.

In fact, it was the first time that he wanted to kiss a girl.

In his dreams there were other girls but he never felt the urgency to kiss any of them. However, Lud was too excited to think about that fleeting (unknown, unjustifiable) desire. He spent the rest of the day and night thinking about that nose. The discovery of that nose empowered him to fantasize – hope, dream – not to take it anymore. All of a sudden the logic of predestination for this taunting was blown to smithereens and for the first time Lud realized all the injustice, the incongruity, the absurdity of that humiliation. And, faced with such an awareness, an unavoidable duty to himself was born. Lud realized that – as he had no alternative except suffering in silence before – now he had no alternative but confrontation. For the first time the word dignity, with all its magnificent fanfare, resonated within him. What a noble sound it had! It was the trumpeting of an elephant, of a hundred elephants! And what color! The purplish red of blood, of fire, of the sun! Dignity, dignity, dignity was reverberating in Lud's brain. He tossed and turned in his bed, was sweating and was being driven crazy by his regret for having failed for so long to be true to himself, by having given up on his *dignity*. Yet, the musicality of this word gave him the audacity that he never had before: getting beaten up seemed like the best price to pay for his dignity, being demeaned, being stomped on. He could see himself dripping with blood, he felt the pain of his broken nose – this made him think about Tom's nose, and he hated him, he hated him! And he saw himself bleeding, but he had his dignity at last. He was deeply moved that he had managed to sacrifice his own blood on the altar of dignity, and he was happy. He couldn't wait until morning, and begged God to help him. He was growling with hatred and venom thinking of Tom, and he cried and repeated to himself over and over *I have my dignity* – and then, in the corner of his mind, he saw Galbanini concerned because he was bleeding on the ground, he saw her caress him and help him get up, and she said to him, "forget about him, Lud, he's an idiot. *You* are the only one with dignity."

At dawn, he finally fell asleep.

In the morning he got dressed in a hurry, didn't drink his Ovaltine, and his mother was worried about that pallor and his cold hands. He looked at her and was on the verge of tears. He was afraid, but the tears that were welling up in his chest were not tears of fear, but tears from the emotion for his own pride in challenging his fear. We could describe his state of mind as heroic. Lud feels absolutely heroic, but this is no laughing matter. He goes on his way with his schoolbag slung over his shoulder and is no longer slouching over, but he is proudly standing straight up, all 4'11." His eyes are no longer stuck on his shoes and the steps he's taking, but focused on the sky, fearless, proud, blue. I look at him and he's beautiful: tenderly, tragically beautiful. He has really changed after this one sleepless night. I don't want to say that he's become aware of his good looks, but he certainly no longer wants to be a little pile of mud thrown into the world, it's time for a counteroffensive. His ego has felt its first palpitation, and when he goes into the classroom he's still a bundle of nerves, but for the first time he has a name. He is a name.

Francesca is seated at her small desk, Lud says hi, Tom and his petulant retinue of Lolitas move closer to him as they usually do: "Hey you freakin' faggot, no one has stepped on you by mistake yet?"

Hearing their bloodcurdling laughter Lud felt like he was buckling under, crushed, humiliated – like an old boxer, cold cocked, all alone, and this time the punches hurt more because Lud knows that they are unwarranted, that he has an obligation to react, and the humiliation is coming from inside, from this new sense of self that he has just discovered and that he doesn't know how to defend, and…

"Hey Tom, don't move that nose, it's creating a draft."

….

Incredible!!! He said it! He said it! He's going to die, but he said it! Courageous kid! He said it like a trembling heifer would have said it on the way to the slaughterhouse, but how proud I am of you! How happy I am for you! Now you are truly very handsome. Tom's eyes were on fire but he – it has to be said – was flabbergasted, the girls froze but after a millisecond of shock they couldn't help but smile, and Francesca's mouth was wide-open and then she laughed like a condemned soul.

What incredible happiness! He had rehearsed every minute detail of this sentence all night, but it was worth it! What a sense of victory!

But there was no time to make a toast because Tom grabbed him by the throat with both hands and lifted him up into the air, showering him with insults and threats. Damn, he had figured and planned on a good belt in the mouth – as a sublime sacrifice to pay for his dignity – but not to be suspended in mid-air wildly kicking his legs! This was humiliating! This was not dignified!

The whole class gathered around them, he was flailing around in the air like Icarus, and then he heard – it was terrible – the tremendous, copious, collective laughter. Finally he came back to earth – the teacher was coming in – and everyone was still laughing.

The humiliation was too much for him, he was running a fever, and stayed in bed for three days, under his smoldering covers, in the scorching warmth of his pain.

But the morning of the third day, Sunday, his mother appeared at his door and announced that he had a visitor. It was Francesca.

Francesca didn't say anything. She took off her bulky parka and scarf and gave them to Lud's mother who said,"I'll leave you two alone."

Francesca was wearing a light colored dress and her stockings were embroidered with lace hearts. She sat on the edge of the bed.

"Does your mother know?" she asked timidly.

"No...."

If my parents knew, they would suffer needlessly because of what *I* did. An impulsive tenderness overwhelmed Francesca and she caressed Lud's face. Francesca suddenly blushed, for that gesture was an imitation of an adult gesture she had seen so many times in movies or felt when her father and mother touched her affectionately: it was a gesture of other people, and for the first time she owned it, feeling all its intimacy and propriety. Lud on the other hand didn't sense the extraordinary power of that caress: it was nothing more than the compassionate patting by his friend who could understand him, and it was done with a gentleness similar to his mother's. "If my parents knew," he continued, "they would understand how ridiculous I am... and petty... a non-entity, yeah, a real nobody."

"Oh, don't say that!" Whispered Francesca, and an involuntary tenderness filled her chest. And when the first tear streamed down Lud's reddened face, Francesca didn't know how to hold back from hugging him, holding him tightly like you would squeeze a wounded puppy.

(There is very little light in the room, Lud's parents went to mass and a silent, sweet perfume is dissipating throughout the house.)

Lud let himself be hugged, he wriggled his hands out from under the covers and then he hugged Francesca, who started crying with him, sobbing nervously. Lud felt all the comfort of that hug and, in a burst of self-pity, he started calling himself lame, an idiot, a chicken shit, then an idiot again because he could no longer come up with any more self-deprecating words but he needed them, because Francesca was still hugging him and crying that no, he wasn't an idiot, no, he wasn't lame....

He was talking complete drivel so he wouldn't spoil that moment of tender warmth, so delicious, so wonderful, and he felt Francesca's tears mixing in with his, and her velvety humid skin pressed against his sweaty cheek, and he clung to her no longer wanting to cry, but wanting only to hold her tightly, ever more tightly....

And Francesca sensed Lud's desires, and she felt a rush of blood rising from her groin to her breasts to her cheeks, she felt like she was on fire and abruptly broke away from Lud. They both looked at each other, disheveled and fiery red, one under the covers and the other seated on the edge of the bed with their sweaty hands intertwined. Francesca pulled up her pantyhose, which had slipped below her knees, Lud started babbling again, something about his being a wimp, so he could hug her once more and feel her slender back with his hands and have her rest her damp face on his. But now, Francesca looked at him without saying a word. She took off her thick glasses and placed them on the night table on the other side of the bed, she stretched over Lud who sniffed all the aromas of her skin and he wanted to have her fragile frame on top of him, and he sensed her breasts, her pale and sweaty skin, he got a whiff of her mouth that had grazed him and didn't know how to plant one on it. Come on Lud! Grab her and kiss her! Your whole body is being inundated by a golden rain of sensations, ever since Francesca hugged you, your small shaft is screaming enthusiastically under the covers – forgetting you're going through a tragedy! And you, for the first time, are feeling the heat of female skin, close to you, and for the first time you realize that Francesca is a young woman, has soft thighs and, surprisingly, breasts....

Then she looks at you and asks, whispering, "can I lie down next to you?"

"Yes," you managed to say.

She took off her shoes, lifted up the sheet, and with the grace of a frightened fawn she slipped in next to Lud. Without looking at one other, they hugged each other tightly under the covers, not understanding what was about to happen. Little beads of sweat were forming on her neck and on his forehead. Francesca bent her head down between Lud's shoulder and the crook of his neck, he smelled her perfumed hair and wanted to do something, but he didn't know what. But they were happy. The silence was so complete to the point of sweeping them away from the present, away from Tom and the laughter of the world, and they were floating, melting like butter, separated from the past and the future, they circled around blissfully in a patch of the universe, freed from the force of gravity as if by some magic spell, left powerless to a sublime and giddy exhilaration...

They are hugging each other to the point of almost not moving, because if they move they are afraid of loosing each other, of slipping out from that embrace, which is at the moment the most beautiful instant that they have ever enjoyed. The shadows are accomplices, so are the tears – but neither one of them is crying anymore – Francesca and Lud have even forgotten their embarrassment, becoming totally absorbed in listening to the infinitesimal, incredible sensations that are coursing through their bodies, and Francesca would like to be kissed and she kisses Lud's neck, and Lud feels a boiling shiver run down his spine liquefying in his pubes, and his genitals – that seem to have been driven crazy by the pleasure – are rubbing against the sheer stockings on Francesca's knee...

And then, who knows how, who knows why, Francesca's thin left arm, surely due to muscle exhaustion, wriggles her way out of the embrace. Lud feels disappointed thinking that was the end of it, but miracle of miracles her arm stops between Lud's chest and his crotch, and Francesca places her tiny hand – like an autumn leaf – there, in an out-of-this-world split second, on the elastic waistband of his pajama bottoms, and Lud heard the birds of paradise shrieking love madrigals in a frenzy and saw the forest iguanas improvising tribal dances…

Lud stopped breathing, hugging Francesca even more tightly. She understood what he wanted, and decided to go for it. She slipped her hand under the elastic, felt the scorching heat, and then she completely possessed his small staff. It seemed enormous to her and she slipped it into the hollow of her hand, lowering her fingers to stroke his boiling testicles. The thought that he was feeling such pleasure by her caressing him and that she was controlling his sensual gratification mesmerized her. It was the first time that she felt like a woman. She felt her mouth full of saliva and yearned for Lud's mouth. She looked up to study his expression and she saw that his mouth was half open and his eyes were closed, in ecstasy. She then realized that she had a big responsibility and firmly grasped his rod moving it up and down and back and forth. She felt its heat in her hand, swelling more and more and getting hotter and hotter, so, intuitively, she boosted up the rhythm – up and down, up and down – until she felt a hot stream shooting from his shaft, spilling onto her hand. She felt happy, and suddenly embarrassed. She took Lud's face in that same hand and kissed it. It was their first kiss.

Then they heard a noise in the front door lock, Lud's parents, she wriggled out from under the covers and tried to straighten herself out, throwing on her clothes, they looked at each other silently, their eyes wide-open, extremely embarrassed that his mom might catch on – but what complicity in that shared embarrassment….

But as soon as they were alone, Francesca in her long coat on the street and Lud still drenched from their under-the-covers' pleasuring, they both relished for the first time the ecstasy of solitude, the revelation that the world is only an appendage, that the world is a déjà vu, an optical illusion … but, of course – envious – let's observe them:

Francesca is moving like she has never moved, still transfixed by the moment, absentmindedly floating, and her only wish is to never go home – and her footsteps are slow, calculated, the footsteps of a young woman. She opens her coat, slips her hands in her pockets, letting the wind bristle her breasts.

Lud, on the other hand, feels discombobulated, he's searching in his head for a shred of what has happened, but it was all so unexpectedly dizzying that there's no memory left of it– and even if he did remember, it was like it had happened to someone else, the only real thing was that kiss, and that kiss was insanely exciting for him.

They both had a blissful and euphoric night's sleep, hands between legs and the sweetest arousal, and as much as they yearned for the next day, they were wishing even more that that night had never ended.

In the morning Lud woke up with a never before seen urge to go to school, to sit next to Francesca, to put his hands on her legs. He came into the classroom, saw her, blushed ferociously, and rushed over to sit down – until he heard a gruff voice, "Well, well, well faggot, does your neck still hurt?"

Tom! Shit, Tom! Who was thinking about him?

Tom stood menacingly over Lud sticking his big nose in his face, arrogantly, humiliatingly, snickering at him. With him were Galbanini and Fiammetta and a tremendous number of who knows who else. Suddenly it returned, even more onerous, even more undeniable, the weight of his own weakness – because he had forgotten about it, damn, he was distraught for a minute, damn, he had been happy...

But then the unexpected happened.

During that horrible concert of laughter, sport, amusement, gums rudely bared and those sharks' eyes arrogantly winking at each other, Lud caught a glimpse of Francesca whose head was bowed, and in the middle of that pack of vultures, I don't know how, he saw the bowed head of his mother and the bowed head of his father. Humiliating the people he loved, and who loved him, triggered something in him that just humiliating him hadn't done: he threw a punch as powerful as a lethal rocket. Or a sledgehammer. Or a train speeding through a tunnel. And Tom fell to the ground. Like a scene in slow motion. Down like a sack of potatoes. Down like a bowling pin or a coconut, two teeth popped out and a shiny gurgling of blood.

(Snap. The noise of broken chains. Silent Stunned Stupefaction. And then, surging from the bowels of the Earth, similar to incandescent lava rising from the volcano – hatred.)

Lud pounced on him with the inhuman ferocity of a wounded tiger, of a thousand bloodthirsty tigers, craving just blood, screaming, "Say that again, tell me what I am!!!" And he shoved his hand down Tom's throat sinking his fingernails right to the back of his tongue, plunging them to his very tender tonsils, to his heart, to inflict the sharpest pain, like some mad surgeon. Everyone tried to pull him off Tom (who was bleeding and whimpering, his eyes dilated in terror) but Lud freed himself from them all with one whack, obsessively screaming, non-stop, "Say it once more, tell me again that I'm a little faggot!!!" Tom, like a horse being slaughtered, was kicking desperately on the ground, gasping for his life (a normal life of stables and prairies), his eyes bulging out their sockets from the pain and the terror of it all, until someone managed to hit Lud on the back (it was the gym teacher, dozens of horrified shouting onlookers had also rushed in) and four of them took advantage of the moment to drag away Lud who still managed to deliver a very powerful kick aimed at Tom's ribs.

People were shrieking, crying, hiccuping, "he's... crazy... he's... crazy". There was a shared sobbing winding its way through the crowd, but Lud was ecstatic, he didn't hear anything, he let himself be pinned down now and was restrained like an enraged doe who has fought to rescue her young and now, tired but satisfied, he just let things be.

His angry tears had dried up, and deep down inside he began to feel the peacefulness of liberation. No one will ever humiliate me again, he was thinking. He was too young to understand that actually no one would ever humiliate the people he loved, that no one should be put down because of him. And he was thinking, What will Francesca think of me? And when he said her name in his head he felt an enormous relief, he understood that he finally had a future. He had never had a future. His tomorrow had always been an obtuse scourge: humiliation. He had a future! He would finally be able to enjoy the sun, the springtime, the pale blue skies, and he pictured himself there (while they were leading him away still holding on to him tightly), he and Francesca gazing at the sky, together on a riverbank by a stream, eating panini together, together.

My God, being happy.

They found serious lesions on Tom's tongue, he needed a lot of stitches, he had two fractured ribs and lost three teeth.

Lud was given a month's suspension from school (not expelled, in light of the testimony of Francesca and some other classmates) and he had to go through the motions of asking for forgiveness, from the principal and the teachers, as well as silently listening to some extremely boring lectures on violence and nonviolence, "It is with dialogue, not with violence, that we can overcome the obstacles that divide us. Violence engenders violence. And is this how you as young men and women will build a new world order?"

But what does the world matter? Lud was completely convinced that to be freed from that slavery, that crown of thorns, he would not resort to any such philosophy. A punch in the mouth. Nothing else. But still, if by chance this wasn't true, why have a dialogue with an idiot? A horrendous malicious moron who, because he was eight inches taller, was allowed to ruin the lives of other students. A punch in the mouth, no other way. Only a belt in the mouth could redeem an idiot. And those four floozies? To hell with them! How could he have had the slightest feeling for that vitriolic viper Galbanini? Even she deserved to be smacked in the face!

And in that moment he wanted them dead – or better yet, tortured, then knocked off. And he thought: that Francesca is alive, is all that matters. My parents and Francesca. Then, when his own parents – whom he had heroically spared from humiliation – insisted that he see a psychiatrist, Lud felt despondent, and the circle tightened even more around him: that Francesca is alive, is all that matters. Tom, Galbanini, Dolores, Fiammetta: let them all croak! The others: whether they live or die – it's up to them!

That Francesca is alive, is all that matters.

About the Author

Emanuele Pettener was born in Venice, Italy, and has lived in the United States since 2000. He teaches Italian language and literature at Florida Atlantic University, where he received his Ph.D. in Comparative Studies in 2004. He has published numerous articles and short stories in Italy and in the United States. He has also published three novels (*E' sabato mi hai lasciato e sono bellissimo* [2009], *Proust per bagnanti* [2013], *Arancio* [2014]) and one book of criticism (*Nel nome del padre del figlio e dell' umorismo. I romanzi di John Fante* [2010]).

He edited a special issue of *Nuova Prosa* 50 (2009): a collection of articles and short stories, entitled "Essere o non essere italoamericani" (Greco&Greco, 2009). With Marco Crestani, he is a scout and editor of the literary blog and publishing company Priamo (http://www.priamoedit. it).

CROSSINGS
AN INTERSECTION OF CULTURES

A refereed series, *Crossings* is dedicated to the publication of translations from Italian to English. Open to all genres, translators should first contact the editors before submitting a complete manuscript.

Rodolfo Di Biasio
Wayfarers Four
Trans. Justin Vitiello
Fiction. $11.00. Crossings 1

Isabella Morra
Canzoniere: A Bilingual Edition
Trans. Irene Musillo Mitchell.
Poetry. $9.00. Crossings 2

Nevio Spadone
Lus
Trans. Teresa Picarazzi
Theater. $7.00. Crossings 3

Flavia Pankiewicz
American Eclipses
Trans. P. Carravetta. Intro. J. Tusiani
Poetry. $9.00. Crossings 4

Dacia Maraini
Stowaway on Board
Trans. Gi. Bellesia &V. Offredi Poletto
Gender. $8.00. Crossings 5

Walter Valeri, ed.
Franca Rame. Woman on Stage
Theater. $18.00. Crossings 6

Carmine Biagio Iannace
The Discovery of America:
Trans. William Boelhower.
Autobiography. $15.00. Crossings 7

Romeo Musa da Calice
Luna sul salice
Trans. Adelia V. Williams
Folklore. $9.00. Crossings 8

Marco Paolini & Gabriele Vacis
The Story of Vajont
Trans. Thomas Simpson.
Theater. $13.00. Crossings 9

Silvio Ramat
Sharing A Trip: Selected Poems
Trans. Emanuel di Pasquale.
Poetry. $14.00. Crossings 10

Raffaello Baldini
Carta canta (Page Proof)
Ed. D. Benati. Trans. A. Bernardi.
Theater. $12.00. Crossings 11

Maura Del Serra
Infinite Present: Selected Poems
Trans. Emanuel Di Pasquale
& Michael Palma
Poetry. $14.00. Crossings 12

Dino Campana
Canti Orfici
Trans. & Notes Luigi Bonaffini
Poetry. $25.00. Crossings 13

Roberto Bertoldo
The Calvary of the Cranes
Trans. Emanuel di Pasquale.
Poetry. $15.00. Crossings 14

Paolo Ruffilli
Like It or Not
Trans. Ruth Feldmann
& James Laughlin
Poetry. $16.00. Crossings 15

Giuseppe Bonaviri
Saracen Tales
Trans. Barbara De Marco.
Fiction. $19.00. Crossings 16

Leonilde Frieri Ruberto
Such Is Life
Trans. Laura Riberto
Intro. Ilaria Serra
Autobiography. $10.00. Crossings 17

Gina Lagorio
Tosca. The Cat Lady
Trans. By Martha King
Thomas Simpson
Novel. $16.00. Crossings 18

Marco Martinelli
Rumore di acque
Translated and edited by
Thomas Simpson
Theater. $15.00. Crossings 19

www.ingramcontent.com/pod-product-compliance
Lightning Source LLC
Chambersburg PA
CBHW050859180626
46814CB00007B/2788

* 9 7 8 1 5 9 9 5 4 0 5 4 2 *